The Lovers' Lane Murders

Secrets of the South, Book 1

Cynthia Hickey

ISBN: 978-1-959788-01-0

DEDICATION

To all those who love a good mystery and seeing justice served.

Chapter One

Pressley Taylor pulled the stack of bound papers from her grandmother's trunk. She couldn't believe she'd found the notes about the murders from over seventy years ago. More surprising was the wooden box inside the trunk that held a small pistol. She'd heard stories, knew her grandmother had tried finding out who had killed her friend, but Pressley didn't really think the notes had been kept. It surprised her more to know her sweet grandmother carried a weapon. It always seemed like an urban legend to her. Grandma was incapable of going after a cold-blooded serial killer as a young woman.

Clutching the papers to her chest, she headed down the stairs of the house she'd inherited. At the dining table where she'd shared many holiday meals, she sat down and started at the beginning, doing her best to decipher her grandmother's scrawling cursive. She booted up her laptop and started typing the notes for easier reading.

February 22, 1946

"Come on, Jean. We've dated for a while. Stop stringing

me along." Danny Harrison put his arm around Jean Daley in hopes of stealing a kiss. "Why do you think I drove all the way out here?"

She placed both hands against his chest and shoved him away. "I'm not that kind of girl." The smile on her face said otherwise, giving him hope.

A twig snapped outside. Her smile faded and her eyes widened. "Did you hear that?"

"Just the sound of my heart beating." He turned her to face him.

"Something's out there," she whispered.

He groaned and pulled away. "You're killing me here." He reached for the key in the ignition. "I might as well take you home if all you're going to do is tease."

The hood of the car slammed up, then down. A large man wearing tan pants, a baggy work shirt, and a pillowcase over his head with holes cut for the eyes, dangled cords in front of the window.

Jean screamed, fumbling for the lock on the door. "Drive, Danny!"

He turned the key over and over to no avail. "Just give him what he wants." He dug for his wallet, tossing it out the window before rolling the window up and locking the door.

Jean's screams vibrated in the car. Fear struck her senseless.

The masked man bent and peered through the window, tapping the glass with a thick stick. His eyes glittered in the light of the midnight moon. He raised his arm and slammed the wood hard against the windshield again and again. Jean shrieked with each hit, pressing her back against the seat.

The glass shattered. He reached inside and grabbed

Danny by the shirt, pulling him across the jagged shards and across the hood, leaving a trail of blood in his wake. Then he turned toward her and put his finger to his mouth, which only caused Jean to shriek louder. "I don't want to kill you, so do as I say."

He dropped the stick and pulled a gun from his pocket, smashing the weapon multiple times over Danny's head and shoulders until the young man lay limp. Jean fought to open her door. When she succeeded, she fell to the ground, then scrambled for the woods.

A hand gripped her hair and yanked her back, dragging her toward Danny's body. The attacker left her a limp heap beside her boyfriend.

"Please, don't hurt me." Tears blurred her vision. Her gaze locked on the gun swinging toward her head.

She woke, her body battered and bleeding. Gripping the grass around her, she painfully dragged herself away from Danny's body. Her assailant watched from the edge of the trees, telling her to run. Sobbing, she struggled to her feet and staggered away.

A car sat at the end of the road. "Help me." She limped forward and froze as the masked man stepped in front of her.

"Why are you running?"

"You told me to." Her voice shook.

"Liar." He backhanded her, knocking her to the ground.

Darkness overcame her again. When she opened her eyes the second time, the man and the car were gone. Jean raced down the road.

A farmhouse shone like a mirage in front of her. Sobs choking her, Jean pounded on the door until a man in a bathrobe answered. "Help me." She collapsed at his feet.

Present Day

Pressley didn't think she'd sleep easy that night. She glanced at a yellowed copy of the *Texarkana Gazette* stuck in among her grandmother's notes. **"Sex Maniac Hunted."** She flipped through the pages of notes. Where did it say Jean Daley had been assaulted?

Had the town dealt with not only a serial killer but a rapist? Not finding the answer to her question, she stood and placed her hands on her lower back. She leaned backward, sighing at the loosening pops of her spine.

Organizing these notes would take some time. Pressley couldn't consider heading to Texarkana to investigate until any facts she found were in order. It would be a wild goose chase otherwise, and she'd receive no help from the local police unless she had solid information to give them.

Pressley couldn't take too long, though. Her job had only given her three months to get her grandmother's affairs in order. She planned on two weeks to go through the notes and formulate a plan to finish what Grandma had started. Could she do that in such a short time? Why not just quit her job and write that book she'd been thinking about? Grandma had left her a nice inheritance. She could take as long as needed.

She rolled her shoulders and poured herself a glass of wine. Hopefully, it would help clear the vision of the attack by the Phantom, the name given the killer by newspapers, so she could sleep.

His first two victims had survived their terrifying ordeal. History informed her those that followed wouldn't be as lucky, one of them being Grandma's friend. Still, Pressley didn't think she would've summoned the bravery needed to discover a killer's identity at the young age of twenty as Grandma had. Yet again, Pressley inherited some of that same backbone or she wouldn't be digging into the murders at the age of twenty-five.

Having grown up on Grandma's stories from childhood on, Pressley had always wanted to find out what really happened. During the reading of Grandma's will, the lawyer had said that Pressley would find what she needed in an old trunk in the attic and that Grandma's dying wish was that her granddaughter pick up where she'd left off.

Pressley smiled. She'd found it all right, and it was a doozy. Excitement coursed through her along with the drink. What if she succeeded where local law enforcement and Texas Rangers hadn't? Imagine the book she could write!

Before she could change her mind, she booked a room in a local bed and breakfast in Texarkana. Pressley might as well leave as soon as possible and continue her research where it had all happened. She didn't have much reason to stay in Applewood anyway.

~

The next morning, suitcases, notes, and laptop packed, Pressley made the three-hour drive to where it had all begun. After checking into the B & B, she unpacked and drove to the location of the first attacks just as the sun started to set.

She doubted things looked the same after so long, but she hoped to get a "feel" of the place. Locking the car, she strolled the path described in the newspaper and tried to envision the fear of a sudden attack while parking with one's sweetheart.

Parking. Pressley had stayed so busy with schoolwork in high school that she'd never gone parking. She hadn't dated much in college either. Her grandmother had instilled such fear in her over the events in 1946 that even the thought of being in a car alone with a boy after dark had made her blood run cold. That fear left her missing out on a lot of teenage activities.

Now, she gripped that fear with both hands, fully intending to face and conquer what had imprisoned not only Pressley's grandmother, but Pressley herself.

She strolled past the side of the road, immersing herself in the events of February 22, 1946. Tears blurred her vision as she heard the screams of Danny and Jean.

Headlights illuminated the area as a vehicle pulled behind her car. She shrank back into the shadows, unable to see the driver because of the lights in her eyes.

"Ma'am?" A flashlight replaced the headlights, then clicked off to reveal a police officer. "I received a report of a strange vehicle. May I ask what you're doing out here alone?"

Pressley put a trembling hand to her heart. "Research." She stepped from the shadows and closer to her car. "I thought you were… well—"

"The Phantom?" A hint of laughter mingled with his words. "You aren't the first to come looking. This isn't the spot. Follow me." He led her a few yards down the road and off the asphalt. "I've heard it happened here. You do know he's most likely dead by now?" He faced her. "Who are you?"

"Pressley Taylor. My grandmother was friends with one of the victims. She left me copious notes."

He nodded. "I'm Officer Jackson Hudson. I'm

familiar with the name from former officers, one of whom was my grandfather. Your grandmother interfered with their investigation a time or two. How's she doing? She'd be what, in her nineties now?"

"Yes, she'd be around the same age as The Phantom if he's still alive."

"Nothing to say he is or isn't." He tilted his head. "Why are you digging this all up again?"

"My grandmother's dying wish was that I find out what happened. I may write a book about it, using her notes. She left enough of an inheritance for me to spend plenty of time searching for the truth." Pressley crossed her arms. "Am I breaking the law by being here?"

"No, just dredging up things best left buried. Go home, Ms. Taylor. Let the dead rest in peace." He turned and marched to his car.

"May I come to the station and ask you questions in the morning?"

"Let it be." He slammed his car door and backed up, turning around in the road before speeding off.

Pressley shrugged. The handsome officer hadn't been pleased at all with her explanation for being in Texarkana. She didn't care. Her goal was to fulfill Grandma's dying wish with or without the help of local law enforcement.

The question was—why wouldn't the police want to solve the murder, no matter how long ago it happened?

Chapter Two

March 24, 1946

Roger Johnson took Paula Wilson's hand. "You don't have to be home just yet, right?"

"What do you have in mind?" She pressed against his arm.

"A little smooching." He grinned.

"I don't know, Roger. What about the attacks a month ago? That guy's still out there." She shuddered, remembering the newspaper article she'd read. "He's a pervert, too. I read he assaulted that girl."

"We'll stay close to the road. No one would dare bother us when someone could drive by at any time. Besides, I bet he was a vagrant traveling through and is long gone by now."

"Okay," she said reluctantly, glancing around the deserted street. Folks had started staying out later when no murders followed close on the heels of the first one, but there still weren't as many people out as usual. "Just for a little while, though. It's Sunday night, and I have school in the morning."

Roger opened the door for her, then hurried to the

driver's side. "I'll make it worth the late hour." He winked and started the car.

True to his word, Roger parked just off the main road, easing some of Paula's worry. She turned sideways in the seat and smiled. "Remember, not too long."

"Just a few kisses." He reached for her, pulling her onto his lap.

They hadn't been kissing long when someone tapped on the window. Paula pulled back and stared into eye holes of a pillowcase. She screamed and launched herself to the passenger side of the seat.

The stranger yanked open Roger's door and dragged him out, forcing Roger to his knees. Paula's fingers slipped on the door handle as tears blurred her vision. She closed her eyes as a shot rang out.

~

Hank Woodrow drove slowly past the parked car, craning to see anyone inside. Not being able to, he stopped and got out of his truck. With a cautious glance around the area, he approached the vehicle. "Hello?" He cupped his hands around his eyes and peered through the window. He shrieked and stumbled back.

A young woman lay dead in the front seat, her head against the far window. A man, wrapped in a blanket, lay dead in the backseat. Seconds later, he sped back toward town and the police.

"They're dead." He sagged against the desk of Officer Hudson.

"Slow down. Tell me what you saw." Officer Clyde Hudson grabbed his hat and gun and stepped around the desk.

"Two young people shot dead." Hank gave directions to the scene. "Right there on the side of the road."

"Lead the way, Mr. Woodrow." Clyde dashed for his car and followed the other man to where a dark Plymouth sat. "Stay in your car," he told the other man as he pulled his weapon and approached the parked car.

He didn't need to check for a pulse on either victim. The gunshot in the back of their heads told him they were dead. He stepped back and shined a flashlight around the ground finding the spot where the male had been killed execution-style before being placed in the backseat of the car.

The roar of an engine broke the night's silence. Clyde stepped into the middle of the road in time to see a black Ford speed away. The killer had stayed to watch the aftermath. The officer returned to his car and called the station. "Be on the lookout for a black Ford, make 1941. Time to call in reinforcements. Get the Texas Rangers here. We've got a serial killer on our hands."

"You sure? You don't think it's too soon?" his captain asked.

"Pretty sure. It's been twenty-one days since the last attack, and this time he killed them. He's escalating." An icy fist gripped Clyde's heart. Would the killer wait another twenty-one days or would he kill again sooner the next time? This crime was far more violent and daring than the previous one. "The victims are parked on the side of the road, Captain. The killer took a big chance at someone driving by and seeing while he killed them. The male victim isn't a small man. His attacker would have to be on the large side to lift his body into the backseat."

"That narrows it down." The captain's sarcasm dripped across the radio waves.

"It's better than nothing. Over and out." Clyde disconnected and went to secure the crime scene after telling Woodrow to go home and not tell anyone about what he'd seen.

~

Pressley sat at a table in the library and pored over old books that mentioned the murders in 1946. Very little was said that her grandmother hadn't already written. Grandma had been as thorough as possible for a civilian. Very impressive for a young college graduate. She'd given up the search when she married and started having babies, but there was still more unknowns she'd left for Pressley to investigate.

The librarian strolled by pushing a cart full of books to be reshelved. "Need any help?"

Pressley rolled her shoulders. "Is there anyone alive that would remember The Phantom murders in 1946?"

"There's a few who come to mind. They all live in the nursing home next to the highway. Mr. Carson, Mr. Marvin, and Mrs. Oglesby, but she has dementia. You'd have to catch her on a good day. Why are you so interested in something that happened so long ago?" Her brow furrowed.

"Just a project I'm working on." Pressley smiled. "I'm fascinated with unsolved crimes."

"Do you work in law enforcement?"

"No, I'm a journalist on vacation." She thanked the woman and turned back to the books in front of her. The most popular assumption of the killer's identity was the car thief. That didn't make sense to Pressley, but the murders had stopped upon his arrest. But why go from stealing automobiles to serial killing?

She leaned toward the same conclusion her

grandmother had, that the killer was a soldier who returned home from the war wounded enough in his head to turn to murder. She straightened in her chair. Maybe he'd suffered a head injury that caused him to turn violent.

Closing the books and leaving them on the table as the librarian had instructed, she grabbed her purse and notes and headed toward the nursing home.

"I'm not sure how much they can tell you," the woman at the front desk of the home said, "but if they're willing to talk to you, I don't see why you can't ask a few questions. Mrs. Oglesby is having a good day. You might want to start there. But, if they say no, I don't want you pestering them."

"I won't. Thank you." She watched as the woman wrote down the names and room numbers on a sticky note.

"Just follow the signs. We have a fairly simple layout. Lunch will be served soon, and the residents don't like to miss their meals."

Mrs. Oglesby was in the first room. Pressley poked her head into her room to see a woman in a housedress watching a game show on television. "Ma'am?"

She turned and smiled. "May I help you?"

"My name is Pressley Taylor, and I'm Mary Ann Warren's granddaughter. She married a Mark Clark."

"I knew a Mary Ann Warren once."

"I'm her granddaughter." Pressley stepped further into the room. "I'm a journalist now. Would you mind if I ask you a few questions?"

"Of course. Sit." She motioned to the one other chair in the room. "It's good to see you, Mary Ann, but you shouldn't be roaming around by yourself. They haven't caught the guy yet, you know."

Just like that, the woman slipped into the past. Pressley decided to go along with her. She might recall more if she thought it was still 1946. "I'm being careful." Pressley sat. "Have you heard any new news?"

"Not since he broke into that couple's house." She leaned close and whispered, "I hear that some of the young men are out looking for the killer themselves. That can't be a good thing."

"I agree. It's too dangerous." She must not have gotten that far in Grandma's notes. "I'd like to find out who killed Sally."

Mrs. Oglesby put a hand over her mouth to stifle a gasp. "Did the fiend get to her too? I think you should let Mr. Hudson handle this, Mary Ann."

"I'm hoping he'll help me." The young Officer Hudson, not the former. "But, the police are tight-lipped on this."

"Of course, they are. The public should stay safely locked out of their way. I daresay it isn't safe for us young people to court anymore. Much better to stay home under the watchful eyes of our parents."

"Who do you think the killer is?"

Her eyes widened. "How would I know? With so many soldiers returning home, businesses up and running again, why it could be anyone passing through."

"But killing every twenty-one days? It has to be a local."

She reached over and patted Pressley's hand. "Find a good boy and settle down. Have babies and leave this to the police."

"Do you think it's a soldier?"

The woman looked shocked. "It couldn't be one of

our returning heroes. Where's your head, Mary Ann?" A bell sounded somewhere in the distance. Mrs. Oglesby grinned. "Time to eat. Will you stay and enjoy a meal with me, Pressley?"

"It would be my pleasure." She waited for the woman to move to a wheelchair, then wheeled her into the hall. "You'll have to show me the way."

"Turn right and follow the hall. Hello, Mr. Carson. This is my friend, Pressley Taylor."

An old man using a walker grinned, a roadmap of wrinkles crossing his face. "You sure are a pretty thing."

"We were just talking about soldiers, weren't we, Mary Ann? Mr. Carson was a soldier, Mr. Marvin, too. Yoo-hoo." She waved at another man who stepped into the hall.

Bowed, he walked without aid. He turned, revealing a jagged scar on his left temple. "There's the prettiest girl in the building."

Mrs. Oglesby giggled and patted her hair. "Such flattery. Come and eat with us, you two. Mary Ann is asking questions about the murders."

"Ah." Mr. Marvin nodded. "She's slipped back in time again. She does that a lot."

"I've noticed," Pressley said. "But I would like to ask some questions about that time, if you don't mind. I'm a journalist writing a book."

"Best to leave that in the past, Miss." His voice hardened. "That was a terrible time."

"We lost some good friends," Mr. Carson said. "We don't want to relive it."

"Who do you think killed those people?"

"They caught the guy. It was that thief." He moved away, muttering and shaking his head.

"Now you've gone and upset him." Mr. Miller glared at her. "I don't think I will join you ladies for lunch." He followed his friend.

"I've never known either of them to be rude before," Mrs. Oglesby said. "Perhaps you should leave and come visit another day when they're in a better mood. See if Officer Hudson is coherent enough to talk to you."

Pressley sighed. "You may be right." She continued to the dining room where she left the woman with her friends and returned to the front desk to sign out. Pressley hadn't been aware the former officer resided in the home. If she had, she'd have gone to him first. She shoved open the heavy glass doors to see Officer Hudson approaching. "Hello."

He frowned. "I wasn't aware you knew anyone here."

"Friends of my grandmother's." She grinned. "Did one of the elderly people commit a crime?"

"No, I volunteer to serve them the midday meal a few days a week during my lunch hour." He narrowed his eyes. "You wouldn't be asking questions and upsetting them, would you?"

"Guilty as charged. The two gentlemen I spoke with weren't pleased, and my grandmother's friend asked me to come another time."

"Look, Miss—"

"Call me Pressley."

"Okay. Those who lived through those months in 1946 don't want to be reminded of that horror. Stick to the books for your information."

"A first-hand accounting would be invaluable. I don't think the killer was ever caught, and I want to prove my theory."

"If he wasn't caught, he could still have family living here. Family who wouldn't want it known that their ancestor was a brutal serial killer. That would put you in danger."

Chapter Three

April 13, 1946

Sally Bradford played the last tune on her saxophone, packed her instrument into its case, and then jumped off the club stage to where her boyfriend, Leroy Yates, waited. "That was a good show, wasn't it?"

"You were the best, Sally." He grinned. "The place was really hopping." He crooked his arm and took her saxophone case in his other hand.

They merged with the others leaving the building and headed for Leroy's car. He stashed the saxophone in the trunk and joined Sally inside, turning with a grin. "Want to hang for a while? I know a safe spot."

"Are you sure? These murders have me worried. The newspapers call him The Phantom."

"There's no such thing as ghosts, Sally. He's a man same as any other. We won't go where those other folks went."

"Well, okay, but just for a little while." Her gut told her they were making a very bad decision. She rubbed sweaty palms down the skirt of her plaid dress. "Promise me, Leroy. Promise me he won't come for us."

"I promise." He gave her a quick kiss and opened the car door. "He must follow people. Otherwise, how would he know where lovers go? We'll make sure no one follows us."

Sally watched over the backseat as Leroy drove them to the side of a secluded road. Not seeing a single automobile, she relaxed a bit. "Don't go any further. I want cars to be able to see us if they drive by."

He reached over and gave her hand a squeeze. "We'll see cars coming from both directions." His arm snaked around the back of the seat. "Relax."

Sally tried to lose herself in Leroy's arms, but the ever-present fear of being watched cast a dark shadow over the romance. "I want to go home." She pulled away.

Groaning, Leroy pulled back.

A masked man appeared on the driver's side of the car and tapped the barrel of a gun against the window. Leroy reached for the key in the ignition as Sally's screams filled the air.

The assailant yanked open the door and dragged Leroy outside. Sally shoved open her door and made a mad dash for the woods. Shots rang out behind her, spurring her on despite the tears pouring down her face. She cried Leroy's name several times before clamping a hand over her mouth and fighting not to make a sound.

She stopped to catch her breath and pressed her back against a tree. The snap of a twig sent her running again. Whimpers escaped her lips.

A few yards away, she caught sight of the masked killer and ducked. When he turned to look in the other direction, she resumed her flight. Which way was the main road? If she could reach it, she might find help.

Oh, God, he was getting closer. Her heart beat fast,

her lungs burned, her legs trembled. She'd never make it. The man would kill her like he killed Leroy. She choked back a sob.

A roosting bird shot from a tree. Sally screamed and whirled. Her stalker stood on a slight rise, illuminated by the moon. If she could see him, he could see her. She glanced down at her dress. The white squares in the plaid pattern glowed like a light.

She switched direction and fought her way through thick brush, finally emerging in a clearing. How far had she run? The area didn't look familiar to her.

A shot rang out. Fire burned through her, driving her to her knees. The last thing she saw was the barrel of the gun pointed at her head and the glitter of a madman's eyes through the slits in the pillowcase.

~

The ringing of his telephone pulled Clyde Hudson from a deep sleep. He fumbled for the handset. "Hudson."

"We've got another one. Someone reported the man, but we haven't found the girl yet." His boss's voice sounded resigned.

They were both dead—that was a given. "Where?" After the chief gave him directions, he promised to be there as soon as he could and swung his legs to the floor.

"I'm calling in the Texas Rangers now."

"Yes, sir. It's time." Clyde shuffled to the bathroom. It was past time in his opinion. They should have had rangers here a month ago if not sooner. "See you in a bit."

Half an hour later, he pulled behind the squad car sitting on the side of the road. Two coon hounds sat a few feet away, waiting for their orders.

Clyde approached the chief who stood over the body of a young man. "Do we have an ID?"

"Leroy Yates. Multiple gunshots to the head. Left the club with his girlfriend, Sally Bradford, around one a.m. She played the saxophone in a band. Her instrument is in the trunk, but there's no sign of her." He glanced toward the woods. "My guess is she fled."

Taking the leashes of the two dogs, Clyde nodded. "I'll radio if I find anything." He gave the command and sprinted after the dogs, barely able to keep up with their pace. Shrill barks filled the night sky.

If they'd called in the Rangers a month ago, would these latest victims still be alive? It was definitely time to put a curfew in place. No one out after dark. Already news reporters flooded into town, dubbing the killer The Phantom and causing mass hysteria among the public.

The dogs' barks changed when they picked up a scent. Clyde found the body approximately two miles from Leroy. Like her boyfriend, Sally had been shot multiple times, her dress up around her thighs. He radioed back to the chief that he'd found her. "Looks like she made a run for it, but he caught up to her. She's dead."

The chief cursed. "I'm on my way."

Present Day

Pressley sniffed back tears. How frightened grandma's friend Sally must have been when she'd fled for her life. More determined than ever to find out who had killed her grandmother's friend, she closed her notes.

One way or the other, she'd get Officer Jackson Hudson to help her. Didn't he want to finish what his grandfather had started? How could he not? Clyde Hudson had spent days—months—trying to catch The Phantom and failed. The truth needed to be told for all those who had fought and died.

She packed the handwritten journal and printed out her typed notes. Maybe if Officer Hudson read what she had, he'd be more inclined to help. Before leaving the house, she called the nursing home only to discover the older Hudson was having a bad day and for her to check back tomorrow. Pressley sighed, grabbed her briefcase, and headed for the police station.

The officer frowned at her through a window and shook his head before meeting her out front. "Miss Taylor, what can I do for you?"

"Pressley." She smiled. "I have something I'd like you to look at."

"Does this pertain to the murders of 1946?" He arched a brow.

"Yes." She kept her smile in place.

A muscle ticked in his jaw. His hazel eyes flashed. "Follow me." He led her to a conference room with an oval table and six chairs. "Please have a seat."

"Am I keeping you from work?" Pressley sat and placed her briefcase on the table. "I can come back at another time."

"I'm sure you could." He sat across from her. "You'd come back again and again until I listened, right?"

She shrugged. "Just take a look at my grandmother's journal. If you don't change your mind about wanting justice, I'll continue on my own. I really would like your help, Officer. This case haunted your grandfather. You can be a part of finding out the answers. Let him go to his grave in peace knowing The Phantom was finally identified." She pulled the journal from her briefcase and slid it across the table.

"Leave him out of it. He's an old man on his deathbed." He opened the journal and skimmed the pages. "I'm impressed. She took better notes than most of those involved." He sat back and crossed his arms. "I'll be honest. I've only read through a few old reports, and that was just out of curiosity. The world today has enough trouble. What good can come from dredging up the past?"

"My grandmother's dying wish is enough for me to pursue this."

"It could be dangerous."

"So you've said. Do you really think The Phantom's family cares one way or the other? Unless they're a big name in this area, it shouldn't matter. Lots of families have skeletons in the closet, Officer." *Please agree to help.*

He sighed. "If we're going to be working together, you might as well call me Jackson."

"Thank you." Relief filled her.

"Only on my off time. I can't shirk my duties."

"I understand." She stood and offered her hand. "I'll make copies of the journal and have them ready when you finish work. Where should I meet you?"

"Shelby's Diner, five o'clock. I'll pay for supper." He escorted her outside to the sidewalk, his expression still grim. "I'm serious, Pressley. Pride runs strong here. You could uncover a coiled snake by digging all this up."

She flashed a grin. "I'll leave it up to you to keep me safe. See you later."

The man exaggerated. Who would care about something that happened over seventy years ago except someone wanting to know the truth? The Phantom would be long dead by now. Even Pressley's kin had a killer in the family. Sure, it happened in the 1800s, but nobody cared anymore. It was just something interesting to mention when people spoke about their ancestors.

Glancing both ways, she crossed the street and headed for an office supply store in order to make copies. She still planned on typing the journal but wouldn't have that finished by the time she met up with Jackson. She leaned on the counter while the employee made the copies.

"These look really old," the girl said.

"1946," Pressley answered. "I'm studying the murders that took place then."

"You should hang around on Halloween for The Phantom Ball. It's an annual thing."

"That sounds a bit macabre." Pressley couldn't imagine celebrating such a horrible event.

"It's a big deal. There's parties, picnics, games…I've always wondered what would happen if someone decided to copycat those murders, you know?" She pressed the button on the machine. "I mentioned that to Mr. Beckett once, and he got real mad."

"Who is he?"

"Someone who knows an awful lot about those events."

Chapter Four

1946

Texas Ranger Gonzales marched into the police station. Five news reporters followed close on his heels. The ranger turned and fixed them with a sharp gaze. "If any of you print anything without my permission, I'll have you run out of town. Got it?" Heads nodded.

Clyde fell into step behind the ranger as he headed for the conference room. The big man stopped in front of the case board and studied the notes and photographs there.

"What's this?" He frowned.

"Some of the young bucks around here are trying to help," Chief Rawlings said. "We've warned them to desist."

"See that they do. They'll run this psycho off before we—" He turned as the phone rang and motioned for Clyde to answer.

"Officer Hudson here." A pawn shop owner informed him that a man came in and dropped off a saxophone. Clyde hung up and glanced around the room.

"But we have Sally Bradford's sax."

"It's worth checking into." Gonzales stormed from the room, leaving it up to Clyde to follow.

"He's all yours," the chief said. "Whatever he needs."

Clyde grabbed his hat and hurried after Gonzales. After questioning the pawn shop owner who, thankfully, kept records, they headed to the address of a local hotel. The manager was more than happy to unlock the suspect's room but informed them the man hadn't been around in the last hour or two.

"Thank you for your help." Clyde stepped into the room and glanced around before heading to the small bathroom. "Sir? Got some bloody clothes in here."

Gonzales glanced into the room. "Bag 'em. We'll wait here for the man to return."

Less than an hour later, a very confused Mr. Roberts entered his room. He glanced to where Clyde and Gonzales sat. "What's going on here?"

"You tried to pawn a saxophone," Gonzales said.

"Yeah, so? I need money to pay for my room."

"Where'd you get it?"

"I played in high school. Mind telling me what you're doing in my room?"

Clyde balanced his elbows on his knees. "How did you get blood on your clothes, Mr. Roberts?"

"I got into a bar fight." He moved aside his hair to reveal a fresh cut. "Am I under arrest?"

Gonzales sighed and climbed to his feet. "No, sir, but with the murders happening around here, we had to question you." He slapped his cowboy hat on his head and left the room.

"Stick around a while, sir," Clyde told the man

before following Gonzales from the room.

"He's not our man."

Gonzales shook his head. "No, he isn't. We're back to square one. If The Phantom strikes again, we won't be able to hold back the panic."

"It's already high." Clyde slid into the driver's seat of the squad car. In the ten years Clyde had worked on the force, he'd never run into a situation of this magnitude. With the return of soldiers from the second war, things had definitely changed in Texarkana. "What's our next step?"

"Curfew. Reward."

"Already done."

Gonzales gave a grim smile. "We set a trap."

May 3, 1946

"Hank, you want a drink while I'm in the kitchen?" Molly Simpson peered around the corner to where her husband sat in his favorite chair.

"Nah, I'm good. It's almost time for bed. Just giving the heating pad a chance to ease the crick in my back." He returned his attention to the newspaper in his hands.

Molly carried her drink into the living room but froze. A man wearing a pillowcase over his head stood outlined in the window. He raised a gun.

Molly's eyes widened and her mouth fell open as he fired twice into the back of Hank's head. She screamed and raced for the phone on the wall, cranked it twice, then yelled police into the receiver.

The man fired again, striking her in the face, then again. She sagged against the wall, blood staining the house robe she wore. Her hand lifted to her face.

"Hank?" Sobs and blood threatened to choke her as the shooter headed for the front door and tore through the screen.

Molly stumbled toward the back where Hank kept their pistol, her hand leaving a trail of smeared blood on the walls. Hearing the man, she switched direction and headed for the back door. Her hands slipped on the door handle. She sobbed and fumbled to open the door as footsteps fell behind her. Finally, she lumbered outside and staggered across the street to her sister's house. When no one answered, she raced to the next neighbor.

Drawing on strength she didn't know she had, Molly continued on, praying, crying—the pain in her face unbearable. She fell onto the Wilson's lawn. "Help me! Hank's dead."

A light flickered on. Mr. Wilson stepped onto the porch. "Who's there?"

"It's me. Molly." She held up a hand and glanced back, screaming as the masked man stopped across the street.

Mr. Wilson darted into the house, re-emerging with a shotgun. "You there! Get out of here or I'll shoot." He fired, kicking up dirt at the man's feet.

The shooter turned and disappeared into the cornfield behind Molly's house.

~

"Got another one." Clyde grabbed his hat and raced from the police station. In the car, he turned to Gonzales. "Not a lovers' lane murder this time. He attacked a middle-aged couple in their home. The woman escaped and made it to a neighbor's house."

"That's not his usual." Gonzales frowned. "Why change things up now?"

Clyde shrugged and turned on the siren, speeding toward the Wilson home. "Maybe he was bored."

"No, he's planning his next move."

Clyde drove to the Simpson home, leaving Mr. Wilson to be questioned by other officers. The body of Hank lay on the floor near his chair where he'd fallen. The front door hung open, the screen cut and peeled to the side. The faint odor of burnt fabric rose from a heating pad on the man's chair.

Blood marked Molly's desperate flight from the house. A husband reading the newspaper, a wife getting ready for bed. It didn't make sense. Was the killer so desperate for victims that he broke into people's houses because no one visited the lovers' lanes anymore? Was the dusk curfew what sent the killer into these people's home?

Clyde moved outside the window where the killer had stood. A flashlight lay at the base of a bush.

"Bloody footprints look like they match prints found at the other murders," Gonzales called through the window. "How much is the reward up to now?"

"Over seven thousand, last I heard." Clyde picked up the flashlight and slipped it into his pocket.

"Mrs. Simpson's purse and jewelry were left untouched." Gonzales joined him outside. "Robbery isn't a motive. It's bloodlust plain and simple. That or the man is sex-crazed."

"We don't have proof that any of the female victims were sexually assaulted." Clyde took one more look around the area. Not finding any other clues, he headed for the car. "Might want to raise the reward. Maybe folks will donate money." He told the ranger about the flashlight.

"Send that to Washington ASAP. Tomorrow, I'll have a press conference. Let's flush this bastard out."

Present Day

Pressley spent the rest of the afternoon printing out and poring over newspaper articles from the spring of 1946. The police had very little to go on back then.

Tips had poured into the station, all of them leading nowhere. She glanced at her grandmother's journal. What secrets were still left to be revealed? Any? Obviously, Grandma had run up against a dead end, too, or she would have turned over her notes to the authorities.

The newspapers mentioned a petty car thief as the murder suspect because the killing stopped when the man was arrested for his crimes. No way it could be that easy. Besides, stealing cars and killing people were two different things.

A glance at the clock had her gathering her things and rushing to meet Jackson. She slid into a seat across the round table from him. "Who is Beckett?"

"The local eccentric." He tilted his head to the side. "His family owns a lot of land around here and has lived in the area for over a hundred years. Why?"

"Because I was told he knew a lot about what happened that spring." She set her briefcase on the floor and pulled out the folder of duplicate copies. "Here you go. It makes for excellent reading."

"What do you think happened?" Jackson's mouth quirked.

"I don't go along with the original assumption of someone passing through once a month. No, I'm certain it was a resident of Texarkana. Fueled by…that's what I'm here to find out. A returned soldier suffering from PTSD seems the most likely." She opened the laminated menu. "Soldiers returning home, new people moving to town, jobs opening up. Yep, The Phantom lived here, chose his victims, and followed them. He had to have been a big man, strong enough to pull those men from their cars. When he no longer had anyone to follow in the nighttime hours, he attacked a couple in their home."

"You should be a cop the way your mind works. Have you read the interview of Mrs. Simpson?"

"Not in any detail. It's in my bag to read tonight."

He laughed. "Great reading right before bed."

"I'm not scared. That particular killer is long dead." She chose a French dip sandwich with fries and a diet soda. From the shadow in Jackson's eyes, she could tell he was worried she'd bring someone to light who didn't want new information found.

He ordered a double cheeseburger and handed the waitress their menus. "I'm off tomorrow, so I'll go through all you've brought me tonight. Once I know what we have, we can make a plan."

"I'd like to speak with your grandfather tomorrow. Will you come with me?"

He sighed. "I'd rather you didn't go alone, so yes."

"What about Beckett? Do you know him?"

"Not really. The man stays to himself. Owns the hardware store."

Pressley suddenly needed a box of nails. Questioning the man at work might be easier if she seemed like a curious tourist rather than someone writing a book. She also didn't want Jackson with her when she asked Beckett questions. The man was bound to know the local police and would put his guard up.

"If my grandfather is coherent tomorrow," Jackson said as the waitress set his food in front of him, "he'll remember your grandmother very well."

"I guess she made a nuisance of herself." Pressley sniffed the savory *jus* that came with her sandwich, then glanced up with a smile. "Kind of like me."

"It's obvious you two share the same bloodline." He laughed and bit into his burger.

At least he smiled at her now instead of frowned. His smile could make the saddest person feel better. Dark hair, thick lashes around hazel eyes, and a dimple that revealed itself only when he truly smiled made the officer appealing to the senses.

"Why aren't you married?" she said between bites.

"Never found the right girl, I guess. Not many want to date a police officer, even in small towns. Do you ever stop asking questions? Why aren't *you* married?"

"Never met anyone I cared to spend much time with." Plus, she'd been obsessed with The Phantom since finding her grandmother's diary and didn't have time to date. "I've got time before the old clock starts ticking. Right now, I have this story to finish."

He shrugged. "I feel the same way about my work. I'm busy, I have a dog, and I own my on home. Life is fine." He narrowed his eyes. "That's why I'm not excited about digging all this up."

"But I've found enough reason to reopen a cold case." She dunked her sandwich into the broth.

"I doubt it will ever be reopened."

"Maybe not, but I will find out the identity of The Phantom, open case or not."

Chapter Five

1946

Mary Ann Warren stood off to the side as Ranger Gonzales approached the podium in front of the police station. To his left, looking very serious, was Officer Hudson. She couldn't imagine the pressure law enforcement must be under. Earlier that morning, she'd heard that over forty officers were trying to catch The Phantom, and they'd gathered from four different states!

"Please refrain from spreading rumors," Gonzales said. "These only take our officers from the main route of the investigation. It's so important that we capture this man that we cannot afford to overlook any lead, no matter how fantastic it may seem. That is how you can best help the authorities."

What had Mary Ann missed while focusing on her own thoughts? She listened as news reporters blurted out questions. She glanced around the crowd. "Wow. The whole country must be represented here."

"Well, sure." Mark Clark grinned, stopping next to her. "The ranger said on the radio last night that every citizen should keep their guns oiled and at the ready.

Some of the guys and I are heading out to Lovers' Lane to try and trap this fiend. Wanna come?"

She frowned. "That's dangerous."

"But we're all armed. Those poor other people weren't. The jerk won't know what hit him."

Gonzales cleared his throat at the podium and raised his hand to quiet the reporters' questions. "Someone knows someone who wasn't where they belonged on the night of the murders. We want every man and woman in Bowie and Miller counties to recall if they know of someone out of pocket on those nights. Persons who have such information and have been withholding it when they should report it are interfering in an investigation. Come forward. All information will be kept confidential. This maniac must be captured. We believe that we are justified in going to any ends to halt this chain of murder. This killer may strike anyone…anywhere. Come forward in the interest of self-preservation."

"See?" Mark nodded. "That's why me and the guys are taking the initiative. The police need our help." He pulled a page ripped from a newspaper from his pocket. "Look what they found at the Simpson house."

She glanced at the photo of a two-cell flashlight. "That's a clue." She'd have to get a copy of that newspaper to add to her notes.

"No fingerprints." He returned the page to his pocket. "So, you comin' tonight or what? Billy's going to wear a dress and pretend to be a dame."

She laughed. "That I gotta see, but I'm staying hidden."

"Don't be a chicken. I'll pick you up at ten." He flashed another grin and loped to where a group of boys stood.

Mary Ann wrapped her arms around the notebook she carried and strolled toward the library. She had some things to think through…possibilities of who the killer might be. A man wearing soldier fatigues passed her, and she smiled at him. His head was down, and one hand was shoved into his pocket, while the other clutched a duffel bag. A few yards away, Mary Ann turned to see him staring after her. She shuddered and increased her pace. He wasn't the first man to watch her—she was pretty, people told her. But the look in his eyes left her chilled.

~

"Got a tip," the receptionist, Marge, called out. "Mrs. Russell said someone is lurking outside her window."

"On my way." Clyde grabbed his hat and dashed out the door, Gonzales on his heels. *Lord, don't let it be another wild goose chase.* Those kind of tips had been flooding the station all day. They needed to be out patrolling the streets at night, not wasting their time.

Mrs. Russell peered between a slit in the curtains when they pulled up. When she made a move to open the door, Clyde motioned her back. If The Phantom was on the property, which he doubted, he didn't need to worry about her coming between him and the killer.

The bushes to his right rustled. With his hand on the butt of the gun on his hip, he parted the branches. A cat sprang out and dashed across the street. Clyde stumbled back, knocking over a trashcan and sending debris across the sidewalk.

Gonzales cursed. "Another false alarm." He waved for Mrs. Russell to step out of the house. "Ma'am, it was a cat. Please. Only call when there's real danger."

"I wasn't going to go out and investigate." Her eyes

widened. "I'm here alone. My husband is out of town on business. What did you expect me to do?" She pulled a gun from the pocket of her robe. "I'm armed but not a very good shot."

Clyde rolled his eyes. "Maybe there's someone you can stay with until your husband returns?"

"No one."

The police radio called in another spotting of a strange man standing on someone's porch as rain dumped from heavy clouds. The good thing about the downpour is it might keep the young bucks wanting to trap the killer at home.

Clyde and Gonzales approached the house of the next call. "Hands up. Stay right where you are." They pulled their weapons and aimed them at the suspect.

"I'm not doing anything except getting out of the rain," the man said. "The bus is late."

The man's small stature ruled him out as The Phantom. "You frightened the home's occupants. Sir, there's a curfew."

"I had to work late, I swear." His hands trembled. "Is that why there's no bus?"

Clyde sighed. "We'll find someone to give you a lift home." He called the station for a volunteer.

"Received a report of someone wearing a mask over on Roosevelt," Marge said. "Someone knocking on the door on Olive, and gunshots over on County."

"Aren't there any other officers available?"

"They're all busy. These are the ones left without responders."

"On our way." Leaving the man on the porch and letting the homeowners know about his reason for being there, Clyde drove with Gonzales to the other calls.

A loose white-faced calf explained the masked man, gunshots were fired because someone thought they saw someone running through their yard, and the knock on the door was a special delivery forgotten about during the day. Hours of work that resulted in no new leads.

"Officer Hudson, would you mind letting me in on what all happened tonight?" Mary Ann Warren, hair dripping from the rain, stepped from behind a bush. Behind her stood Mark and his gang. "I'm writing it all down so future generations will know what happened here."

Could the night get any worse?

"Wonderful." Gonzales stood right behind her. "I'm recruiting you to be a decoy."

~

Jackson picked Pressley up after breakfast the next morning. "My grandfather is lucid today, but we'd better hurry. Sometimes, he slips fast."

"I appreciate this." Pressley slid into the passenger seat and clicked on her seatbelt. Hopefully, Mr. Hudson would have something new to tell her, and she'd also have another opportunity to speak with the other men and Mrs. Oglesby.

They signed in at the front desk before Pressley followed Jackson to a room at the end of the hall. He knocked, then opened the door. "Grandpa?"

"Come in, boy. It's been a while." An elderly man in a wheelchair turned from the window, a smile gracing his wrinkled face. "Who's your pretty friend?"

"This is Pressley Taylor. I believe you knew her grandmother, Mary Ann."

"Ah, yes. An intelligent but nosy young lady. How is she?"

Pressley held out her hand. "She passed recently, sir."

A cloud shadowed his features. "Too bad. She was a pesky young thing but had a good head on her shoulders. I already said that, didn't I? Sit, please." He motioned toward a small love seat across from him. "I'm guessing you're here to ask me some questions, and my grandson is here to make sure you don't tire me out, am I right?"

"Yes, sir." She smiled, then glanced up at Jackson.

"Why do you think The Phantom was never caught? Did he leave town?"

Mr. Hudson rubbed his chin. "The murders stopped after the shooting of Mr. and Mrs. Simpson. A man stole a car, went to jail, and the murders stopped. After three months, the case was closed. We'd gotten our man, or so it seemed."

Pressley leaned forward, her gaze intent on the old man's face. "You don't think so?"

"No. I think the killer simply got scared and stopped. The town was overrun with law enforcement, folks were more vigilant, carried weapons…it became too dangerous for even a serial killer in the town of Texarkana. Whatever drove him to kill had eased. I always thought him a local man."

"I do too." Pressley tapped her foot. Finally, someone who believed as she and her grandmother did. "Any ideas?"

He grinned, clicking his false teeth. "If I did, I would have arrested the man. Whoever it was, had too much to lose by getting caught. He killed for the thrill of it, then backed off. That's my opinion at least."

"My grandmother thought it could have been a shell-shocked soldier who returned from the war."

"Yes, she told me that, and I agreed at first. The town was full of returning soldiers. But, there didn't seem to be any evidence to support that theory. " He exhaled long and deep.

"You getting tired, Grandpa?" Jackson's forehead creased.

"My head's getting a little foggy. I think it's time to rest. Why don't you two go speak with Carson and Marvin? They were both soldiers returning home at that time. Maybe the years helped them remember something."

Jackson stood and helped Mr. Hudson to the bed. "We will. Someone also suggested Mr. Beckett."

"The man who owns the chain of hardware stores? He's crochety. I doubt he'll say a word."

Once Mr. Hudson was comfortably in bed and the lights dimmed, Jackson headed for the cafeteria with Pressley. "All you got today was validation for your opinion."

"It's enough for me to know that the officer on the case at the time believes the same as I do. The Phantom never left Texarkana." She wished Jackson would have been more interested in the criminal history of his hometown. If he was, he might show more interest in trying to solve the cold case. "Don't you think it weird, though, for a serial killer to suddenly stop killing? I mean, it's a sickness, an obsession, something they enjoy."

"Maybe someone who knew him discovered he was the killer and forced him to stop."

Pressley halted suddenly. "That has to be it. We find the family, we find the man, we find the reason. You're brilliant!"

"Finding out his identity has always been the hard part. I don't understand how you think you can accomplish something others couldn't."

"Because I'm more pesky than my grandmother." She grinned.

A slow smile spread across his face. "That's what I'm afraid of."

Laughing, Pressley linked her arm with his. "Come on. Let's go talk to some retired soldiers." Someone had to know something they didn't realize they knew.

They located the two men playing checkers. Neither looked thrilled to see Pressley but welcomed Jackson.

"She's roped you in, hasn't she?" Mr. Carson said. "I thought you were a stronger man."

Jackson chuckled and straddled a chair. "Might as well humor her."

"Ha ha, gentlemen. We've spoken with Mr. Hudson, and he recommended we talk to you again." Pressley pulled up a chair. "May I?"

Nods and sullen looks gave the answer, but no one asked her to leave.

"Mr. Hudson and I believe The Phantom may have been a soldier returning from war. How can I find out who came home?"

"Military records, I reckon," Mr. Marvin said. "Or, I can write them down for you. I remember the face and name of every returning soldier." He crossed his arms. "It breaks my heart to think one of those fine men could have murdered those people."

"I don't like to think so, either," she said. "But, it's something we need to look into. When can you have the list?"

"You got a pad of paper and something to write with

in that purse of yours?"

Half an hour later, the two men, conversing between themselves, added and eliminated names. Now that Pressley had her list, it was time to investigate each of the names.

Chapter Six

Mary Ann slouched in her seat next to Mark. In another lane through a stand of trees another decoy couple sat in wait, one of them a boy in a dress. She shook her head. They were all out of their minds. The silly ploy wouldn't work.

"Wanna smooch?" Mark wiggled his eyebrows.

"Be serious. We aren't out here to fool around." She rolled her eyes. If they didn't keep their wits about them, they could die. Images of what could be flashed through her mind. Gunshots, torture, rape. What was she doing out here?

Mark took her hand. "I won't let anything happen to you."

"I'm sure the other girls' boyfriends told them the very same thing." She peered through the window into the moonless night. It would be easy for someone to sneak up undetected. She'd talked brave about wanting to hunt down The Phantom, but when the Ranger recruited her and Mark, her first thought was to back out at once.

"There are officers in the trees, Mary Ann. What could go wrong?"

"I don't see anyone."

"That's because they're at Spring Lake Park and we're here on the side of the road. They'd be here in less than five minutes." His voice echoed his growing frustration. "I didn't think you were such a scaredy-cat."

"Only a fool wouldn't be frightened out here," she whispered harshly.

Gravel crunched outside.

"Shh." Mark's brow furrowed. "Get your gun."

"It's never left my hand." She tightened her grip.

A flashlight blinded her right before a tap on the window. "What in tarnation are you two doing out here?" Officer Hudson asked. "You shouldn't be here alone. The stakeout is at the park."

"You're lucky we know you." Mary Ann sat up, her heart racing. "I could have shot you." She showed him her .25 ACP pistol.

"God spare me from young people venturing into foolishness."

"The killer won't go near the park with all those people," Mark said. "He ain't stupid. Somebody had to stake out away from the rest."

"No, he might not be stupid, but you are." The officer shook his head. "Go home. Now."

Relieved, Mary Ann didn't argue. She'd stick to asking questions and taking notes. Stepping into danger wasn't her forte. Maybe investigative journalist wasn't the career she should pursue. Maybe she should listen to her mother and get married and have babies.

"Always on the weekends, always late at night," she muttered. What drew him to commit such atrocities?

"Evil strikes at night," Mark said, starting the ignition. "Easier to hide under the cover of darkness."

"It has to be a soldier."

His gaze jerked her way. "What makes you think so?"

"He's real good with a gun. I mean, most folks around here have guns, but he's sneaky. No one sees him or hears him until he's right there striking to kill. Remember, the first victim—the one who survived—said the man was a wacko. Said some really strange things."

"That psychiatrist who gave an interview doesn't think he's military. Said his warped mind would have been discovered. He also said the killing would stop because it would become too difficult to commit the crime."

"Why not move to a different town?"

Mark shrugged. "That's the question we might never find an answer for."

~

"Ready to talk to Beckett?" Pressley asked as soon as they were inside Jackson's car.

"Sure. What about this list?"

"I'll have to find out who has living relatives still around before formulating a plan. Can you help with that?"

"I'll make a copy of the list and send it to the station receptionist. She can research it while we're with Beckett."

After a quick stop at the photocopy shop and after sending the list to the receptionist, Jackson drove Pressley to a renovated brick storefront. "Last I heard, he keeps his office in the back of the first hardware store they built. A symbol of pride for him, I guess. Let's hope he's in."

A few minutes later, they were ushered into the luxurious office of Frank Beckett, owner of Beckett's Hardware. They sat in leather chairs across from the man at his polished desk, the hard glint in the man's eyes not making them feel welcome.

He folded his hands on a spotless desk blotter. "Officer Hudson, how may I help you?"

"I'm actually here with Pressley Taylor on unofficial business. She's writing a book on what transpired here during the spring of 1946 and was told you were the person to ask."

Beckett's eyes narrowed, and he turned to Pressley. "Why would you want to drag all that up again? Let the dead rest in peace."

She forced a smile. "My grandmother's best friend was one of the victims. During that time, my grandmother took copious notes. It was her dying wish that I finish the story."

"I wasn't around then, and my grandfather has been dead for a long time. I doubt I have anything to tell you that wasn't in your grandmother's notes."

Pressley's heart sank. She'd put a lot of hope in this stern man to give her some answers. "Your grandfather never talked about that time?"

"No. Why would he? Some things are best left forgotten. It's bad enough we celebrate every Halloween like it's a joyous time. It didn't even take place in the fall. By then, things were over and the killer dead behind bars, so they say." He leaned forward. "I suggest you let it be and make up an ending if you don't believe the dead-in-jail theory. I've a busy day ahead. Please see yourselves out." He offered a thin-lipped smile.

Pressley stood, gripping the handle of her briefcase

hard enough to make her fingers ache. "Thank you for your time." Back straight, she marched from his office, through the store, and outside. She took long, even breaths and counted to ten. Of all the rude people she'd ever met, Beckett won the prize.

"Are you okay?" Jackson asked, joining her on the sidewalk.

"He didn't even consider helping us."

"Come on. Let's get lunch and see if my receptionist discovered anything for us."

She nodded. Dwelling on disappointment wouldn't get her anywhere. "I am hungry."

"I know a diner where you can get just about anything you want." He opened the passenger side door for her. "Don't worry about a man like Beckett. We'll find our information somewhere else."

They stopped by the station first after receiving a text from the receptionist, Marge, saying she'd put the list through the database and had their information.

"Slow day so got right on it." Marge smiled and handed them two copies of what she'd discovered.

"Let's get lunch to go and head to the hotel so I can use my laptop."

"Even better, we'll grab a sandwich from the coffee shop and use their Wi-Fi. I'm sure it's better than that rundown motel." Jackson grinned. "I've a laptop in the car. With both of us researching, we'll be done in half the time."

Thrilled he seemed to be fully onboard with her now, she agreed and glanced at her list. "Funny how Beckett's name is on here."

"Why is that funny?"

"I'm imagining digging up something juicy on him

that will propel him to talk."

Jackson laughed. "You have a mean streak, don't you?"

"Only when warranted."

Pressley ordered a sandwich and large fruit tea at the coffee shop and immediately logged onto her laptop. She'd search for relatives of the 1946 returning soldiers while Jackson focused on criminal records of those same soldiers. A killer wouldn't have a completely spotless record, would he? Wouldn't there be at least an assault charge or something?

"In my grandmother's notes," she said, "a psychiatrist didn't think it could be a soldier because that kind of mentality couldn't be hidden."

"We didn't know as much about sociopaths back then," Jackson said without looking up from his computer. "We now know how easily they can fit into society without detection."

True. She would stick with her gut feeling of a poor man suffering from what they called PTSD in the present. Pressley still couldn't get over how the murders had suddenly stopped, but maybe the reason would be revealed along with other answers.

"Ooh, Beckett's grandfather spent time in an insane asylum during the time of the murders. I guess that rules him out as the killer." Pressley sighed.

Jackson grinned. "I was kind of hoping the killer belonged to the Beckett family."

"Now who's being mean?" She arched a brow.

"It would be nice to bring the man down a rung or two. The Becketts have acted high and mighty for a very long time."

Pressley slowly turned her head to the left, then the

right to release the tension, and reached for her tea. "Something doesn't add up, though. His grandfather returned from the war and was immediately sent to the hospital? If he had mental issues, wouldn't the military have taken care of him? When did he have time to settle down and have a family?"

"Good point. The current Beckett wouldn't be here if his grandfather hadn't married. Try to find a marriage certificate."

"The war ended in September 1945, and the murders didn't start until the following February. Frank Beckett the Second returned from duty during the Christmas season of 1945 and married his high school sweetheart immediately upon his return. But, the hospital shows him admitted at the same time. A clerical error?"

"Possibly. I'm not finding any behavior problems or arrests for the man."

"Okay. Let's look at the other names." She filed Beckett away in her mind to dwell on in more depth later.

By the time they finished, they had five people still living in the area who had relatives alive during that time. All soldiers coming home. It was a good place to start. *Grandma, we're going to solve this for you. I know it.*

~

He watched them from the other side of the coffee shop, secure behind a fake tree. At least hidden enough he wouldn't be noticed. What were the two of them digging up? Who cared after more than seventy years?

Why would they want to smear someone's name now? Because some old woman wished it? Because an old man in a nursing home couldn't solve the case all those years ago?

He gulped his coffee, burning the roof of his mouth and increasing his anger. Cursing, he stormed from the shop, glaring at people he passed by. The last thing he needed was for his peaceful life to be disturbed by a nosy woman who didn't even live in Texarkana.

Laughter compelled him to glance over his shoulder. The officer and woman strolled down the sidewalk as if they were lifelong friends. His eyes fell on the briefcase in the woman's hands. If the cop wasn't with her, he'd leap forward and grab it, stealing her notes to find what she'd discovered.

Even better, he'd hire some thug to break into her hotel room. That would be safer and make sure he wasn't a suspect in the theft. Mood improved, he shoved his hands into the pockets of his suit pants and headed home to his submissive wife and pit bull, Lee—the two living things he could always count on to do what they were told.

Tomorrow, he'd pay old Officer Hudson a visit.

Chapter Seven

June 28, 1946

Clyde drove past a mostly vacant parking lot, slowing by a car reported stolen the night of one of the murders. He parked behind a short wall and waited, hoping someone would come and claim the vehicle. It didn't take long before a woman left a corner store and slid into the driver's seat. Clyde, hand on the butt of his weapon, approached the car. "Hands where I can see them, ma'am."

"What did I do?" She put her hands on the steering wheel.

"Are you aware this is a stolen vehicle?"

"It is?" Her innocent expression didn't ring true with him.

"Please, get out of the car." Clyde took a couple of steps back.

"My name is Paige Sweeney. I just got married in Shreveport. My husband is in Atlanta, Texas. He's the one who stole the car, and he's there to steal another one." The woman rambled, spilling her guts. "He travels around to make it harder to get caught. Please. I didn't steal anything.”

“You knew you were driving a stolen automobile.” Clyde cuffed her.

“Yes, but—”

The radio on Clyde’s belt crackled alerting him to the fact a man tried to sell a stolen car to a dealer but vanished when the shop owner confronted him. Clyde called for backup to retrieve Mrs. Sweeney. When another officer arrived, he handed the woman over and headed to the car dealership.

“Would you recognize the man who tried to sell you the car?” he asked the owner.

“Yes, sir. Wore a cowboy hat and boots. Told me he needed money to leave town because he’d committed a horrendous crime.”

Cowboy hat and boots fit a lot of people in town. “Mind coming with me to see if you can spot him?”

“Sure. Let me lock up. Do you think he’s The Phantom?”

“No way of knowing at this time, sir.” Clyde gave a thin-lipped smile and led the manager, Mr. Davis, to his squad car.

After visiting a few public places and not seeing the man, Clyde led Mr. Davis to the bus station. They strolled through the crowd, studying every man in a cowboy hat and boots. One man turned, his eyes widening, then bolted from the building.

Clyde gave chase. When the man tried to climb the fire escape behind the building, he grabbed his ankle and yanked him down. Planting his knee in the man’s back, he cuffed him. “Mr. Sweeney, by any chance?”

“Yeah. Don’t shoot me.”

“You’re under arrest for car theft. Why would I shoot

you?" He pulled the man to his feet and marched him to the backseat of the squad car.

"Don't play games. You know I'm wanted for more than stealing cars."

After dropping Mr. Davis off at the car lot, Clyde headed for the police station, hoping he'd finally obtain some answers.

After booking the man, he led him to an interrogation room. "Sit. Can I get you something to drink?"

"Coffee," Sweeney muttered.

Clyde took his time getting the small cup of tepid coffee. He wanted the man to sit and worry for a while. After half an hour of watching Sweeney through a one-way window, he entered the room and set the now cold brew in front of him. "How long have you been stealing cars, Mr. Vern Sweeney?"

"Only recently. I need to make some quick money to leave town." He wrapped his cuffed hands around the cup.

"Why's that?" Clyde sat across from him.

"I don't want the electric chair."

Clyde froze. "Why would you get the chair?"

Vern slowly raised his head. "Because I killed those people."

"Really?" Clyde crossed his arms. "Can you tell me why?"

"There's something wrong with me."

Of that, Clyde had no doubt. "Will your wife back up this story of yours?"

Sweeney nodded. "I told her all about it."

"Yet she stayed with you."

"Love is crazy."

Not as nuts as the man sitting across from him. "I'm

going to lock you up now and go question your wife. Is there anything else you want to tell me?"

"No." Vern sipped the cold drink and grimaced. "That's the worst coffee I've ever had."

"Sorry, this isn't the Ritz." He motioned through the window for someone to escort the suspect to a cell and went to move the wife from her cell to the interrogation room. "We've arrested your husband," Clyde told her, taking the same seat he'd sat in when talking to Vern. "He says he killed some people."

"He's The Phantom. Vern told me so. How did you find out?"

"Why didn't you mention that when I arrested you?"

She shrugged. "I didn't want to be next. I was close by during one of the murders. You'll find my footprints near where Leroy Yates was killed."

Clyde rubbed his hands roughly down his face. She'd watched a man being brutally murdered and done nothing? Didn't make sense. Plus, any footprints were long gone.

Chief Larson rapped on the door. "Got a minute, Hudson?"

"Excuse me." He joined the chief in the hall. "Yeah?"

"Sweeney's prints don't match any of the ones found at the deaths or the Simpson house. Not even on the flashlight." He shook his head. "The car registered to them was spotted parked under a bridge the night Yates was killed. They're nothing more than attention seekers. Book Sweeney on car theft and let the woman go with a warning." He groaned. "We're getting all kind of loony confessions. It's enough to drive me batty."

This whole case was one big mess from the very

start. Clyde stormed into the interrogation room and removed the woman's handcuffs. "You might want to leave town. Once people find out the game you were playing, they may not be very friendly toward you." As for himself, Clyde wanted to wring her neck and lock her up with her husband.

~

"Do I know you?" The old Officer Hudson frowned.

"No, sir, I guess you don't." He sat and crossed his right ankle over his left knee. Since the man didn't recognize him, today must be an off day, and he'd get no information out of him. He fingered the fringe on the throw pillow next to him. Now, he wasn't sure whether he should go through with his original reason for visiting or not.

What if the old man remembers and tells his grandson he visited? He'd worn sunglasses and pulled his hat low, leaving a fake name at the front desk. No one would know his identity easily, but they might remember the last man to visit Officer Hudson before his death.

Without another word, he pushed to his feet and rushed from the building, not stopping until he stood in front of the motel where Pressley Taylor rented a room. He'd called earlier that morning and found out she was on the second floor, room 202. It paid to be a man of some worth in town. People said things they wouldn't with someone else.

The curtains in that room parted, then fell back into place a few minutes later. He didn't worry. She might see him standing there, but he was too far away for a positive identification. He wanted her notes and laptop but could wait. He was a patient man when he needed to be. It wouldn't do any good to have Officer Hudson acting in an official capacity because of a robbery. No, the loss of her things needed to look like an accident or a street mugging.

Shoving his hands in his pockets, he whistled as he strolled away.

~

Pressley studied the man across the street. Something about him seemed familiar, but then again, she couldn't place where she might have seen him. With all the wandering around town and questioning people, she figured she'd seen him in passing. She shrugged, let the curtains fall into place, and returned to the small round table in her room.

Now that it was past nine a.m., it was a respectful time to start making phone calls. The first on the list was to a woman who lived a few blocks away, according to the internet.

Pressley dialed the number. "May I speak with Mrs. Mayes?"

"If this is a telemarketer, I'm going to hang up."

"No, ma'am. My name is Pressley Taylor, and I'm writing a book on the murders of 1946. I've discovered you had a family member return from the war during that time. May I ask you some questions?"

"I'm not sure what I can tell you, but I have a few minutes."

"Did he seem okay to you when he returned?"

"A bit shell-shocked, but that's to be expected, right?"

"Did he have any other relatives?"

"Why, sure. We're first cousins to Frank Beckett. My maiden name is Beckett." She lowered her voice. My great uncle, Roy, the soldier…well, he disappeared right about the time when those murders stopped."

Pressley's heart skipped a beat. "And?"

"Folks around town speculated that his father sent him to the asylum up there in Little Rock. I'd suggest you speak with him, but he's been dead now over five years. Have you questioned Frank?"

"Yes, ma'am. He's a bit reluctant to talk with me."

"Of course, he is. If word got out that The Phantom was a relative of Frank's, his reputation would be ruined. You know how small towns are."

"Thank you, Mrs. Mayes. You've been helpful." Pressley hung up and chewed the end of her pen.

Experience had taught her that small towns thrived on gossip and drama. She seriously doubted Frank's business would suffer. More likely people would flock to the hardware store in search of information.

What should be her next move? Her grandmother's journal had stopped with the disappearance of The Phantom. In order to complete the task set before her, she'd have to use every investigative trait she might have. Grabbing her purse and locking her room door behind her, she strode to the police station to speak with Jackson. She marched to his desk. "I need a ride to the asylum."

He glanced up with a grin on his handsome face. "Lost it already?" He tapped his temple. "You made it so easy."

"Very funny." She sat in the chair across from him and told him of her phone conversation with Mrs. Mayes. "Can you drive me or direct me to someone who can?"

"I'm off tomorrow. I'll drive you, but I'm not sure what good it will do. The asylum kept horrible records in 1946. Anyone who knew Roy Beckett will be long gone."

"The retirement home still holds a few who remember. I can talk to them again, but I still want a ride to Little Rock."

He shrugged. "Suit yourself. I'll pick you up at nine a.m. tomorrow."

"Thank you." She stood and turned to leave, then returned her attention back to Jackson. "Someone is watching me. There was a man staring at my window earlier."

That caught his attention. "Could you tell who it was? What did he look like?"

"Dark sunglasses and a cap pulled low over his eyes. But I might be paranoid—you know, ready for the asylum." She didn't think she was paranoid, though. Pressley had learned a long time ago to trust her instincts.

Jackson glanced around the empty room and sighed. "I can't leave. I'm the only one here. Call me the second you reach your room." He stared at the clock. "Ten minutes."

She gave him a salute and hurried to her room, resolved to spend the rest of the day locked away.

Chapter Eight

Jackson knocked on her room door at five minutes before nine. "Did you sleep well?"

"I did." She smiled and invited him in. "There's coffee if you'd like a cup."

"I have a thermos in the car but thanks."

Pressley took another sip of hers, grabbed her laptop bag, then followed him from the room, locking the door behind them. "It's only a couple of hours drive, right?"

"Yep. Did you learn anything else from the journal?" He opened the car door for her, then jogged to the driver's side.

Pressley shook her head, climbed in, and clicked her seatbelt into place. "It's done but not complete. Her pages stopped with the deaths. The last thing she wrote about was Sweeney and a lot of false confessions. She gave up, got married, and had babies."

"Too bad that wasn't the end of the story."

She cut him a sideways glance. "As a police officer, I'd assume you'd want to find out what happened to the killer."

"A lot of time has passed." He pulled onto the interstate. "I'm sure my grandfather would be more enthusiastic if he weren't ill." He smiled her way. "But, you're pulling me in."

"Good." He had been willing to help. She'd be glad for any assistance he gave. "Are people here really willing to risk everything to cover up what a relative might have done?"

He laughed. "Oh, yeah."

"Then we should pay Frank Beckett another visit."

"That's a good idea, despite the fact he won't tell us anything. You would make a good detective, Pressley."

"Thank you. I prefer the journalist aspect of crime. I'm not into the whole facing bad guys thing."

"Keep digging and you might face one. Years ago, some of the asylum's cooks were charged with the murder of forty-seven inmates. They put poison in their food. You might have a better chance solving that crime than this one."

"This crime was my grandmother's dying wish."

Two hours later, they pulled into the drive of a sprawling red brick building complete with turrets. "Impressive and eerie."

Inside, they approached a nurse sitting at a desk behind a glass partition. "May I help you?"

"We'd like to speak to someone who might know of a resident here in 1946." Jackson slid his badge through the opening in the glass.

"We don't have any employees here from that time, Officer."

"The director, maybe?" Pressley refused to be turned away so quickly. "We only have a few questions. Anyone with access to records can help us."

The nurse frowned. "Wait here." She returned a few minutes later with another nurse. "Nurse Reynolds is in charge of the facilities records."

"How may I help you?" The middle-aged woman with kind eyes smiled.

Pressley explained they were trying to find information on a Roy Beckett, a World War II veteran. "We're looking into why he was here."

"Follow me, please." She buzzed them through a heavy door and led the way down a long hallway to a room full of file cabinets. A few minutes later, she slid a folder across a table. "This is all we have on the man with that name, but it isn't much, I'm sorry to say."

Pressley sat in a hard chair and opened the file. The records stated that Roy Beckett had been brought to the facility by his father for shell shock and violent behavior. Roy died there a few years later. Nothing to confirm her suspicions that the man had been The Phantom. Jackson was right. It was a waste of time.

"You don't have anything on his behavior and state of mind while a resident here?" She glanced at the nurse.

"As a violent man, he would have been sedated to the point he was no a danger to anyone." The nurse crossed her arms. "We have one resident who might remember that time period. Let me check with his doctor to see if he's capable of answering any questions. He's ninety-four and doesn't always make sense." She left them in the room, returning a few minutes later. "He hasn't had his medication yet, so he's coherent." She stepped back while a thin man leaning heavily on a walker entered the room.

"This is Vincent Gray. Mr. Gray, these folks would like to talk to you. I'll be right here if you need me." She sat in a chair beside the door.

Mr. Gray cast a wary look at Jackson, then took a

seat across from him and Pressley. "What do you want? It's almost time for lunch."

Pressley smiled. "Do you remember a man named Roy Beckett?"

His forehead creased. "Yeah. Crazy as a loon."

"Did the two of you ever talk about the killings that took place before he arrived here?"

"Sure. Roy said he killed those people. That's why his father sent him here. Why would he lie?"

Pressley glanced quickly at Jackson, then back at Mr. Gray. "Do you think he killed those people?"

"He knew everything about it. How he followed them, what he did to them, even the color of the robe the woman who escaped wore. Of course, he did it."

"Why weren't the police told?"

"Roy was already locked up here. What good would it have done to put him in prison?"

"Did Roy read the newspaper?"

"Religiously." Mr. Gray laughed. "Roy was a bit of a celebrity after his confession."

Pressley sighed. All the information Roy had spoken about could easily have come from the paper. Just because Roy had confessed didn't mean he was The Phantom. Plenty of others had confessed to the same crimes, only to find out they'd lied.

~

Nosy woman. Frank sat in his car a few spots over from where Taylor and Hudson had parked. He'd suspected more nosiness when they'd left town that morning. What he hadn't expected was to follow them here. How had they found out about Roy? Only Hattie would know about him.

This was not good. Not good at all. His grandfather

had to be rolling in his grave. The family name would be dragged through the mud. All of his childhood years, the fact they had to keep Roy's insanity and violence a secret had been drummed into Frank's head. He wouldn't let one nosy woman ruin it all.

Frank slumped in his seat as the two returned to their car, then followed them back to the interstate. He needed to formulate a plan to get rid of them. One that would deflect their attention off Roy and onto someone else.

As Frank drove, he came up with the perfect plan and couldn't wait until nightfall. More than one Beckett could strike fear into the hearts of Texarkana. He'd keep the police too busy to help Pressley stick her nose where it didn't belong. But first, he had to take care of Hattie.

~

"I'd like to check on my grandfather if you have time." Jackson glanced at Pressley whose pretty face was creased from thinking about their visit to the asylum.

"All I have is time."

"What's wrong?"

"I'm not convinced Roy is our guy. I mean," her frown deepened, "it's a strong possibility, but other than his say-so, we have no definite proof."

"I'll try to pull some strings and see if I can't get DNA. We have resources now that weren't available back then."

Her face brightened. "That's a great idea."

It surprised him how good it felt to cheer her up. *Get a grip, Jackson. She won't be staying in town long. Pressley has a life outside of Texarkana.*

They signed in at the retirement facility and made their way to his grandfather's room. "Grandpa?"

Recognition dawned in his eyes. "Jackson, my boy.

It's good to see you so soon. Weren't you here yesterday?"

"No, sir. Did you have a visitor?"

His brow furrowed. "I think so. He left quite promptly. This morning, I had the feeling I knew him so figured it was you, and I was having a bad day."

Jackson would check the prior day's sign-in sheet. His grandfather rarely had visitors other than him, and he'd like to thank the person. "Feel up to a conversation about 1946?"

His grandfather frowned. "Why are you bringing that up again? We've already discussed it."

"My apologies, sir," Pressley said, pulling up a chair, "but we just came from the asylum where Roy Beckett allegedly confessed to another inmate that he had committed the murders. What I don't understand, though, is the last time we talked, you mentioned this, but the dates don't match up. If Roy had been committed immediately upon returning from the war, he couldn't have committed the crimes."

Grandpa shrugged. "Dates on records are messed up all the time. Roy isn't the first person to confess. I see you're still stuck on the returning-soldier theory."

"It makes the most sense to me, sir. Sweeney died in jail, but there was no evidence to support him being the killer. Roy seems likely, but the dates don't match." Her shoulders slumped. "Maybe this is a dead end. Maybe the killer simply disappeared in the swamps, never to be seen again."

Grandpa patted her hand. "That's a theory that would never be proved. I wish you luck, dear girl. I have a feeling if anyone can get to the bottom of this, it'll be you and my Jackson. It would be nice to know the truth before I die."

That did more to make Jackson want to proceed with helping Pressley than anything. It could be the last thing he did for his grandfather…identify The Phantom.

When his grandfather showed signs of tiring, Jackson led Pressley to the front desk and asked to see the register. He flipped to yesterday and noted a David Morris had signed in to see his grandfather. Jackson didn't know of a David Morris in town.

"Do you remember this man?"

The young woman at the desk nodded. "Your grandfather doesn't receive visitors other than you."

"Did you recognize him?"

"He seemed familiar, but he never looked straight at me. Wore his cap pulled low over his face, signed the book, and hurried down the hall. Is there a problem?"

Jackson handed her his business card. "Call me if he shows up again, please. I'd like to thank him for his visit." A cap pulled low. Could it be the same man who had watched Pressley's window? He glanced back toward his grandfather's room. Was he safe, or was someone worried about the facts locked in an old man's mind?

"What is it?" Pressley put a hand on his arm.

"It appears someone is not only watching you but my grandfather as well."

"Is he in danger?"

"I don't know." He turned back to the woman at the desk. "Actually, I would prefer no one visit except myself. It puts a strain on him."

"All right." She wrote on a purple post-it note and tacked it to a board above her desk. "Done. Can I help you with anything else?"

"That's it." Jackson flashed a grin, then put a hand on the small of Pressley's back, liking the feel of it, and led her from the building. "I'll see about pulling the DNA and prints from Roy Beckett's medical records and let you know what I discover."

"Thank you. I'd like to find out one way or another if he's the man we're looking for. If not, we can focus in on another direction."

Which direction? If Roy wasn't The Phantom, they had no other leads.

Chapter Nine

Frank watched from the bushes as an older model Chevy parked on the lane and turned off its lights. He'd wait until the young couple inside lost themselves in each other before making his move. His hand clutched the butt of his pistol. Was this how Roy had felt in the seconds before making a kill? Excitement coursing through his veins like a drug?

The car window rolled down and the girl giggled. The moon shone through the back, illuminating the two in the front seat. The young man leaned in for a kiss.

Should Frank shoot them outright or play with them first like a predator toyed with its prey? Already, he fed on their fear and knew tonight wouldn't be the last time he killed. He was hooked.

Once he felt certain he wouldn't be noticed approaching the vehicle, he pulled a ski mask over his face, grabbed the tire iron he'd laid on the ground, and then stepped from his hiding place. He slapped the hood of the car loud enough to make the couple jerk upright.

The young man scrambled to lock the doors and roll up the windows. Frank grinned at his vain attempt to protect himself and the girl. He'd anticipated such a move and broke the front window with the iron. While the girl's screams vibrated against his eardrums, he pulled the man through the now empty windshield.

"Please, don't hurt us." He held up his hands. "We'll give you anything you want."

"I want your life, boy." Frank raised the tire iron. "Once again, Texarkana will fear sundown." He brought the iron down on the man's head, once, twice, a third time until he lay still. Then, Frank turned back to the car.

The front passenger door hung open. So, history would indeed repeat itself. With a chuckle, he went on the hunt. Frank hadn't gone far when another car door opened. He turned in time to see the girl slide from the backseat and sprint for the main road.

Today's youth were smarter than those in 1946, it seemed. No matter. He raised his pistol and took aim. The bullet struck the teen in the center of her back. Whistling, Frank headed to where he'd hidden his car.

~

Jackson listened to the radio in his car in disbelief. A young couple killed on Lovers' Lane. He turned on his siren and raced in that direction.

A copycat? It had to be. The Phantom would be too old now, if he were even still alive, to overpower two healthy young people.

Ten minutes later, he stood over the body of a young girl. One shot to the back. The beam of his flashlight shone on her date lying a few feet away. On the other side of the road, another young couple huddled together. Jackson headed their way.

"You found the bodies?"

The young man winced. "Yeah, we were, uh, looking for a place to park and…"

Jackson knew why they were there. "Why don't the two of you head home now. Come to the station in the morning to fill out a report. You don't need to be here any longer." They'd already seen too much. "Don't tell anyone what you've seen here. Not until we have a chance to notify the next of kin. Do you know these people's names?"

"Yeah, I play football with Josh. That's his girlfriend, Tammy."

"Thank you." Jackson returned to the scene to wait for the chief to arrive.

He didn't wait long. Chief Rawlings arrived without flashing lights or a siren, pulling up behind Jackson's car. "A damn shame," he said, glancing at the girl's body. "Any signs of the perp?"

"I haven't searched yet." Not that he expected to find much. The area was popular with the high school group and there'd be a lot of footprints and tire tracks. Jackson skirted the area, studied what he could, and snapped a few photos with his phone. He didn't have much to go on. It was easy to see which tracks belonged to the dead couple since their car still sat there. The blood on the shards in the windshield showed how the young man had been pulled from the vehicle.

Just like in 1946. "Chief, we have a copycat of The Phantom. Should we implement a curfew?"

"And start a panic? Let's not jump the gun here, Hudson. Could be a transient."

"That's what they thought back then." He shook his head. His gut told him there'd be more deaths before too long. If they had a true copycat on their hands, they had less than a month before he struck again.

He found a set of footprints a few feet into the forest.

The footprints went in, turned, and came back out. Here's where he'd waited for his moment. Jackson followed the prints, finding where the killer had stood and taken aim at Tammy. It wasn't much, but it was something. He put his foot next to the print. So, the man wore a size eleven.

"Find something?" the chief called.

"Size eleven footprint. Common tread on the soles, though."

"Reporters are here. Hold them back. We don't need them contaminating things."

Jackson nodded and retrieved a roll of crime scene tape from the trunk of his squad car, tying it around trees well away from Tammy's body so the arriving reporters couldn't get too close.

"Do you have identification on the victims?"

"Is The Phantom back?"

The reporters shouted questions and thrust microphones and cameras in his face. "We don't know much at this time. The chief will hold a press conference when we do." Jackson turned and marched away from their eagerness. He had a long night ahead of him.

~

Pressley woke to a knock on her hotel door. She peered through the peephole to see Jackson, still in his uniform. "What happened?" She opened the door.

"A double homicide." He entered the room and headed straight for the empty coffeepot. With a sigh, he tore open a pack of the supplied grounds and started a pot. "Done in the manner of The Phantom."

"What?" Her legs failed her, and she plopped into a chair. "He's too old."

"I know."

"You don't think it's a one-time killing, do you?"

He faced her. "What are the odds that we start asking questions about the murders in 1946 and an almost identical murder takes place tonight?"

How could this happen? "This is my fault." All she'd wanted was to fulfill her grandmother's dying wish.

"No, it isn't." Jackson handed her a cup of coffee and poured another for himself. "You had no idea what would be triggered."

"You suspected. That's why you were hesitant to let me disturb things here." She turned the cup around and around in her hands.

"Hey." Jackson took the cup from her, set it on the table, and then clasped his hands around hers. "A horrible thing happened, but it was not your fault. We'll catch the guy who did this. Things are different now than they were when The Phantom terrorized this town. We're better trained and have more ways of catching the bad guys."

His words didn't help. The young couple died because she'd brought up the past. Tears stung her eyes.

"Oh, sweetheart." Jackson knelt in front of her, keeping ahold of her hands. "I don't know what else to tell you to make it better."

"There's nothing you can say." She sniffed.

"I have to go to the office and do paperwork. Why don't you come with me, and I'll buy you breakfast when I'm finished."

She gave a sad smile. "Grandma always thought food would make things better, too." Pressley pulled her hands free and rose to her feet. After dressing in a pair of jeans and a loose-fitting tee shirt, she put her hair into a messy bun, grabbed her laptop bag, and followed Jackson to his car.

"Wait here," he said when they reached the station. "I won't be too long, I hope."

She sat in one of the waiting chairs. Before she could open her laptop to scan her grandmother's notes, a young couple, visibly shaken, entered the station and approached the receptionist.

"We're here to fill out a report," the young man said. "We're the ones who found the bodies."

"Please have a seat, and I'll let Officer Hudson know you've arrived."

The teenagers gripped each other's hands and sat in the empty chairs near Pressley. The girl glanced her way with red-rimmed eyes.

"I couldn't help but overhear," Pressley said. "I'm a friend of Officer Hudson. He told me what happened. I am so sorry."

"Thank you." The girl's voice barely rose above a whisper. "It was horrible."

"Did you see anyone around? A car maybe?"

She shook her head. "Just Josh's car and his and Tammy's…bodies." She shuddered and covered her face with her hands. "I'll never forget that sight."

"We did hear whistling," the young man said. "I just remembered. But, we didn't see who whistled."

"Whistling?" Jackson stepped in front of them. "From which direction?"

"The end of the road opposite where Josh had parked."

Jackson glanced at Pressley, then motioned for the teens to follow him to his office. "I'll be right back."

She doubted that and pulled out her laptop while she

waited. The bell jingled over the door again. This time Frank Beckett entered and demanded to speak with Jackson. The quick glance he sent Pressley chilled her to the bone.

"Seems you and Hudson are inseparable." He sat in the chair next to her and crossed his arms.

"Hello to you too, Mr. Beckett." She closed her laptop. "Jackson and I are friends. He's helping me."

"Right. Helping you snoop where you don't belong. Why don't you go home?"

"I'm not finished here." She met his stony gaze with one of her own. "Why does it bother you so much that I'm here? I'm no threat to you."

"Shows what a stupid thing like you knows." He jumped to his feet when the chief entered the room. "I heard about the murders. What do you plan on doing about it? We don't want a repeat of 1946."

The chief's face darkened. "How did you find out, Mr. Beckett?"

"Police scanner and a reporter."

He muttered something about stupidity. "We'll do the same as we would in any situation of this kind, sir. We'll investigate and apprehend. Excuse me." The chief turned and marched back to his office.

"Watch your back, Miss Taylor." Beckett stormed from the station.

That sounded very much like a threat to Pressley, and she wasn't one to back down when pushed around. She turned to stare out the window as Beckett strode down the sidewalk. He stopped at the corner, sneered, and tossed her a wave, then crossed the street toward his hardware store.

Not only had she caused the deaths of two young

people, but she'd riled one of the town's upstanding citizens. She used upstanding loosely. Beckett might be influential, but he was anything but a nice guy.

When Jackson escorted the two teens from his office, the receptionist called out to him. "The prints and DNA results have been sent to you."

Jackson grinned. "Come on, Pressley. Let's take a look before going to breakfast."

She followed him to his office and leaned over his shoulder while he checked his email. The heady scent of his aftershave dispelled the uneasiness Beckett had left behind.

"Well, look at that." Jackson tapped his screen. "Roy Beckett was The Phantom. You fulfilled your grandmother's wish after all."

Pressley smiled. "Let's keep this a secret until we catch the copycat."

"We?"

"You need me. I have all the notes from that long-ago time. There's a clue in there somewhere that will help us now."

Chapter Ten

Pressley had stayed up late the night before studying her grandmother's notes for anything she might have missed. Way too early in the morning, she sat up in bed. "Frank Beckett." She snatched her phone from the bedside table and called Jackson.

"Hello." A groggy Jackson answered. "It's four a.m."

"Sorry. I know who killed the young couple the other night."

"All right. You have my attention."

"Who has the most to lose when it gets out that Roy Beckett was The Phantom? Frank. He killed those kids to keep the police force occupied."

"How do you know this?"

"Because I've spent months reading Grandma's notes. I know how a psycho thinks. Yesterday at the station, he told me to watch my back."

"He threatened you?" Jackson sounded awake now.

"Seemed that way to me." She flung off the blankets. "We need to pay him a visit."

"Not this early. We'll have to wait until his store opens. Beckett won't try anything with people around.

I'll pick you up a few minutes before nine. Go back to sleep." He hung up.

There'd be no more sleep for Pressley. While the brew perked in the coffee maker, she paced her small hotel room. Frank couldn't know they'd discovered Roy had killed those people. He had to believe Pressley still searched for the truth. Had he really snapped enough to start a killing spree again?

She wasn't a psychiatrist. Maybe it was more than shell shock that sent Roy off the deep edge. Mental illness ran in families. Roy's father had to have been off in his mind to falsify the date he had committed his son. Pressley poured coffee into a mug and carried it to the window. Her arrival in Texarkana had been the trigger to set Frank off, once again confirming it was her fault the latest victims died.

The window and the cup in her hand shattered a breath before she heard the gunshot. She dropped to the floor and crawled to the other side of the bed, grabbing her phone off the table.

"Someone shot at me through my window," she said as soon as Jackson answered.

"On my way. Make sure your door is locked. Hide in the bathroom." Click.

Pressley army-crawled to the bathroom and locked herself inside. Since her room was on the second floor of the hotel, no one could gain access to her room except through the door. She'd be fine. All she had to do was breathe. Jackson was on his way.

What if the shooter picked him off when he arrived? Pressley needed to do something. But what? She didn't have a weapon. The twenty-two pistol lay at the bottom of her bag in the other room. Not that she knew how to shoot it. Maybe Jackson could give her lessons. She huddled on the floor, wrapping her arms around her bent knees.

"Pressley?" Jackson pounded on the door of her room.

She'd never been so glad to hear Jackson's voice in her life. She raced from her hiding place and let him in. "Thank God you're okay."

"Me?" He put his hands on her shoulders and peered into her face. "I'm not the one someone shot at. Are you okay?" His gaze dropped to her hand. "You're bleeding."

Blinking in surprise, she glanced down. "The coffee mug must have cut me when it shattered. It didn't hurt until now." Now it throbbed with a vengeance.

"Come on." He led her to the bathroom and told her to sit on the toilet lid. "Let me bandage this up, then I'll scout around outside. Did you see anyone?"

"No."

He poured disinfectant over the wound, clucking his tongue at her hiss. "You don't need stitches, but a butterfly bandage would help staunch the blood. Then, I want you to get dressed and packed while I take a look around. You're staying with me until this is over." He gave her a quick kiss, seeming as surprised as Pressley at the act, then rushed from the room.

Putting her fingers to her lips, she locked the door after him and smiled. If that peck on her lips thrilled her so much, what would a real kiss be like?

After a quick shower, she packed the few items and made another cup of coffee. Anything to keep her mind off Jackson. Since no more shots had rung out, the shooter must have left. That didn't make her worry any less.

She jumped to her feet when Jackson knocked and announced himself again. "Find anything?"

"Size eleven footprints. Same as the site of the murders. Ready?" He glanced at the suitcase on the bed, then lifted it, leaving Pressley to grab her laptop bag. "Let's get you checked out. I'll have to go to the station next to let the chief know what happened here."

The spontaneous kiss seemed to have made him uncomfortable, if the fact he avoided her gaze was any indication. Why did men have to be so weird?

~

How could he have missed her? Frank cursed and punched the dashboard.

That meddlesome woman had discovered the truth about Roy. If the records clerk at the police headquarters to whom Frank paid money to keep her mouth shut hadn't called him about the fingerprints, he'd still be ignorant as to what Pressley and Hudson had discovered.

Getting rid of them would accomplish nothing now other than making Frank feel better. He also no longer had a reason to copycat Roy. Except…he smiled…he'd liked the power he'd felt at taking their lives.

Going home or to the store was too risky now. It didn't take a genius to know the new terror stalking the town was Frank. He might as well enjoy striking fear in people's hearts as long as he could. But there'd be no waiting. He'd find his next victims that night.

Frank headed to the bank and withdrew as much money as allowed, bought supplies at the local supermarket, and made a quick trip home. He threw clothes into a suitcase, grabbed his computer and hard drive, then headed to a hunting cabin deep in the woods. He'd hide out there as long as was needed.

Maybe, instead of killing Pressley outright, he'd grab her and take her to the cabin for a little fun. Roy had sexually assaulted some of his victims, as the rumor went, so why shouldn't Frank enjoy that extra benefit?

~

Jackson couldn't believe he'd kissed her. What happened to his resolve not to get involved with her? She'd leave town once things were safe. No, he needed to keep things professional. Her first call that morning had annoyed him. He wasn't a morning person on the best of days, but her second call had scared the hell out of him. Pressley waited in his office while he went to speak with the chief. He knocked on the open door. "Sir, do you have a minute?"

"Sure. Have a seat." The chief settled back in his chair, his eyes widening as Jackson told him of the attempt on Pressley's life. "I'm taking her home with me."

"Smart move. I'm going to find someone to take your place here until this is over. You are now a bodyguard."

Jackson scowled. "You're removing me from the case?"

"Not at all. You seem to work well with this woman. Find Frank Beckett and bring him in for questioning. Keep Miss Taylor and yourself safe in the meantime and keep me informed."

"You're agreeing to use a civilian to catch this killer?"

The chief shrugged. "She found the identity of The Phantom, didn't she? None of the authorities were able to. Why not use that sharp mind of hers? Whoever the killer is—and it might very well be Beckett—he has a grudge against Miss Taylor. He'll come for her. That's when you nab him." The chief grinned. "You should let your grandfather know. That's news he will want to hear."

"Yes, sir." Jackson retrieved Pressley from his office, not liking the fact the chief wanted to use her as bait. "Time to talk to Frank."

The man wasn't at his store or at his residence. Apparently, taking the time to talk to the chief had allowed the man to vanish. Jackson clenched his teeth hard enough to send pain into his jaw. There was no way of knowing where he'd fled to, but Jackson would bet his favorite shirt the man was still close enough to continue to wreak havoc.

"We need to alert the media." Pressley put a hand on his arm. "Frank will kill again. The people of this town need to be warned." She dug in her bag and pulled out a pistol, setting it on the dashboard. "I'd like you to teach me how to shoot."

Jackson's eyes widened. "You are full of surprises. Let's visit my grandfather, then I'll take you to the shooting range."

It was another good day. His grandfather grinned when Jackson told him about Roy. "I knew it. If only we'd had the evidence back then, we could have prevented the deaths of a few kids. Good job, you two. I can die in peace now."

"Not anytime soon, I hope." Jackson gripped the old man's hand. "We believe Frank Beckett is picking up where his relative left off."

Grandfather frowned. "Why? There are years between the two of them. Frank is what, forty-five maybe? Roy would have to be ninety-four if he'd lived long enough. I was only a few years older, the youngest detective on the force. What would killing gain him?"

"Revenge," Pressley said softly. "My arrival triggered whatever madness lurked in his soul."

"Never mind that, young lady. Your grandmother would be so proud. You have the same tenacity Mary Ann did."

"I take that as a great compliment."

"As you should. Now shake off the foolishness that this is all your fault and help my grandson find this madman."

"Any idea where he might have gone?" Jackson asked.

"Not a clue." He shook his head. "I'd guess he's holed up on some long-forgotten family property. Maybe the courthouse would have records of his holdings. I wish I were young enough to do this with you. All the excitement has gone from my life now."

"You'll have to get it secondhand." Jackson pushed to his feet. "I'll see you tomorrow."

"Looking forward to it."

Pressley leaned over and planted a tender kiss on his grandfather's cheek. "I'm glad to have met you, sir."

Jackson's heart warmed at her gesture. The glow in his grandfather's eyes said he felt the same.

"Take care of our girl, Jackson."

"I will." He liked the sound of her being their girl. So much for resolving to avoid a relationship. His mind said one thing, but his heart was shouting something different.

Once they were back in the car, he placed a call to the chief to let him know there was no sign of Frank. "We should alert the media, sir."

"I agree. I'll take care of it now. The people of Texarkana will be kept informed of the danger and alerted to the possibility of a curfew. I won't implement one immediately. I'm holding onto the hope that Beckett is long gone. But if he isn't, I'll slap down a curfew so fast it'll make your head spin. We will not have a repeat of 1946."

Jackson was afraid that was exactly what was going to happen.

Chapter Eleven

"Do you want to get settled in my guestroom first or go shoot?" Jackson glanced her way.

"Shoot." She grinned. "It's a skill I'll need before long." She wasn't sure her attempt at humor worked.

Jackson's brow lowered. "I hope you won't, but yeah…you'll probably need to know how. The chief believes the killer will come for you."

Her blood chilled. "Do you agree?"

"Unfortunately, and it scares me to death."

He surprised her by returning to the station. "The safest place for you to practice shooting is where I do."

Made sense. It was best to keep her out of sight until she could defend herself. An outdoor range would leave her vulnerable.

After an hour of target practice and gun safety, Jackson handed Pressley the target sheet. "You're a natural. Hit the kill zone seven out of ten times."

"I want ten out of ten."

He laughed. "We'll practice more later. I want to head to the courthouse and see what property Beckett owns." He glanced at his phone. "After we go check on

Grandpa again. Someone tried to visit him."

"Beckett?"

"I don't know. The receptionist refused to allow the visit, and the man left."

They raced to the retirement facility only to find out the visitor had been a reporter hoping to question Jackson's grandfather about The Phantom. Pressley glanced down the hall in time to see Mr. Carson being wheeled from his room. At her wave, he motioned her forward.

"How are you, Mr. Carson?" She smiled down at him.

"Concerned is what I am. Come eat lunch with me and the boys. We've some things to discuss." He waved away the assistant. "You push," he told Pressley.

"Let me tell Jackson where I'll be." She returned to the front desk.

"That's fine. We'll eat here." He thanked the receptionist and took over wheeling Mr. Carson to the dining room.

Lunch consisted of canned green beans, a roll, and a grilled chicken breast with rice. Pressley hated anything canned and shoved aside the beans.

"You don't eat vegetables?" Mrs. Oglesby asked, taking a seat at their table.

"Not green beans." Pressley smiled and welcomed Mr. Marvin who had joined them. "The whole crowd's here."

"We always take our meals together, dear." Mrs. Oglesby patted her hand. "Some days, Mr. Hudson joins us, but I heard he's having a bad day today."

Concern creased Jackson's forehead. "Our conversation yesterday may have tired him too much."

"No, he was more excited than he's been in a long time." She smiled. "We had quite the conversation ourselves. You telling him about Roy was a good thing. Now, Mark," she said to Mr. Carson, "why don't you tell these young people what you remembered?"

He nodded and stabbed at a green bean. "Roy Beckett returned from the war on the same bus as me and Marvin here. He seemed agitated and kept glancing at a letter he held in his hand. We suspected it might have been one of them Dear John letters, you know?"

Pressley glanced at Jackson. "The trigger?"

"Maybe. If a woman he loved broke up with him upon his return, he might have taken revenge on other young lovers."

"Why not just go after her?" Pressley leaned forward.

"Well, that's the thing," Mr. Carson said. "He dropped the envelope. When I picked it up to hand it back to him, I noticed the postmark said Colorado. His girl had moved away. Most likely with a new bloke."

"You didn't catch the name on the return address, did you?" Jackson asked.

"Didn't have a name. Just an address I didn't have time to read."

That might explain Roy's motive. Pressley picked at her rice. A shell-shocked soldier facing rejection from the girl he'd left in the states. A tragedy for so many innocent people.

"You two believe Frank Beckett has taken up where Roy left off, don't you?" Mr. Carson glanced from Pressley to Jackson. "Why would he?"

"Because I dug up the past," Pressley said.

"Not your fault, girl. Evil would have been exposed

somehow even if you hadn't shown up."

Maybe. But her arrival might have sped things up. "There aren't any more Becketts to take over in a few years, are there?"

"No one left but Frank and his cousin."

The woman who gave them information on Roy. Pressley gripped Jackson's hand. "We need to check on Mrs. Mayes. If Frank figured out that she spoke with us, she could be in danger."

"I agree." He shoved back his chair and sprang to his feet. "Let's go. Thank you for your help, folks."

"Anytime."

Pressley scribbled her phone number on a napkin. "In case you remember anything else." She turned and hurried after Jackson.

In the car, she looked up the woman's number and placed the call. It rang and rang but didn't go to an answering machine. "No answer."

Jackson's expression grew graver. Pressley didn't think it possible his features could harden more than they had over the last hour.

"I'll get her address from the station." A few minutes later, they sped to the far side of town.

~

Jackson pulled up to a small white house with aluminum siding and overflowing flower beds. Several days' worth of newspapers lay on the walk leading to the house. Not a promising sign.

"I suppose it's a waste of time to ask you to stay in the car?"

"Considering people die in their cars, yes." Pressley shoved open her door. "Besides, I'd wonder what was happening the whole time." She pulled her gun from her bag. "Thanks to you, I now know how to use this."

"But can you shoot someone?"

"Hopefully, I'll never have to find out."

He hoped so, too. Shooting another person left a mark on the person who pulled the trigger. A mental mark that never went away. Jackson pressed the doorbell, then knocked when no one answered. A few minutes later, he turned the doorknob. The door opened.

The smell of death made him stagger back a few steps. If not for the danger to Pressley, he'd have ordered her to stay on the porch.

"Oh, my." Pressley pulled the neckline of her tee shirt over her nose. "I'll, uh, wait right inside the door, if that's okay."

He understood her reluctance to see a decomposing body. Swallowing back bile, he moved through the house, locating Mrs. Mayes in the kitchen. She'd been tied to a chair with dishtowels. A single gunshot between the eyes. Written in her blood on the table were the words, "Talkers die."

Returning to the front room, he pulled Pressley outside, having her stand behind a porch post. It would offer some protection if Frank were watching. Then, he radioed the chief, letting him know what had happened.

"I'm calling in reinforcements," the chief said. "Things are going to escalate fast once the media hears of this." He cursed and hung up after muttering about there being nothing new under the sun.

Jackson hoped the chief would implement a mandatory curfew immediately. Not that everyone would comply, but most would, and that meant saved lives. He stepped onto the lawn. Where are you hiding, Beckett?

"Let's visit the courthouse," He said after the crime scene techs showed up. Since he wasn't working in an official capacity, having been relegated to investigating on his own, he had no reason to stay and oversee things. The other officers could handle it from here. Keeping a sharp eye on their surroundings, he led Pressley back to the car, then drove into town.

The courthouse didn't reveal any holdings other than Frank's house and his stores. Next stop, a warrant to visit each of those. Something he most likely wouldn't obtain until the next day. He might as well take Pressley back to his place. Having this beautiful woman living under the same roof would make staying an arm's length away difficult. Every time he looked at her, he remembered the feel of her lips against his. His gaze landed on her mouth. A strong urge to give her a stronger kiss, to wipe away the fear he saw in her eyes, flooded through him. Yep. It would be difficult to keep his distance.

"I hope this is okay." He opened the bedroom door to reveal a queen-size bed with a plain blue comfortable. "I'm not much for interior design."

She laughed. "This is fine. It looks more comfortable than the motel mattress."

He set her suitcase on top of the bed. "Pizza okay for supper? Neither of us finished our lunch."

"Sounds great. Anything but anchovies." She smiled, drawing his attention back to her lips.

He cleared his throat, nodded, and rushed from the room as if a swarm of hornets were after him. Idiot. Focus on the job and on keeping the two of them alive. Figure out how to catch Frank before he killed again. Stop thinking about Pressley!

Safely away from her room, he ordered a large mega-meat pizza and a liter of diet soda and another regular. He'd forgotten to ask her what she preferred to drink but refused to enter her room again. Dangerous territory for a man who hadn't dated in far too long. Work took up most of his time, and a lot of women couldn't deal with dating an officer who faced danger on a regular basis.

When Pressley joined him, he sat on the sofa and watched the news. Bad choice. He should have chosen the chair because she plopped down right next to him.

"Any news about Mrs. Mayes?"

"Top story. The media is calling Frank The Second Phantom. That didn't take long."

"No, it didn't. At least they aren't aware yet that Frank is officially a suspect."

"I hope it stays that way for a long time. Catching him is going to be hard enough as it is."

~

Frank watched from his car as a young man still in his basketball uniform, his arm around a pretty little blonde, headed for a beat-up Ford Taurus. Hopefully, they wouldn't head straight home but would take a detour.

He eyed the gun on the passenger seat. The desire to kill gnawed at him like a rat on cheese. Strange how quickly he'd become addicted to the act. Now he craved the fear he caused.

Good little children. They turned onto the road heading toward the lake. Lovers' Lane wasn't the only place for teens to go parking.

Frank parked in the trees, then set out on foot. He'd come across the couple he'd followed or someone new.

It didn't make any difference to him. A kill was a kill. A scream, a scream.

Pulling his ski mask low, he stepped from the woods. The couple had left the car and spread a blanket on the lake's shore. How romantic. Gripping his gun, he moved forward.

A twig snapped under his foot. He froze.

The young man lunged to his feet, hands balled into fists. "What do you want?"

"For the two of you to strip naked. Then, you get in the water, chest high." He might as well make things fun. "I plan on having a good time with your girlfriend."

The girl screamed and scrambled off the blanket.

The boy rushed toward her, grabbing her hand. "Help us!" he screamed and pulled the girl into the trees.

Nice. A hunt lay before Frank. He grinned under his mask and whistled. They weren't hard to follow. The couple made enough noise for a deaf man to find them. Frank narrowed his eyes when a road appeared through the trees. The couple made a mad dash and flagged down a vehicle. Frank raised his gun and fired, striking the young man before he melted back into the shadows. There was still plenty of hours left in the night.

Chapter Twelve

Jackson's phone rang shortly after midnight. Two seconds into the call, he lunged from the bed, raced down the hall, and banged on Pressley's door. "Get up. He struck again. Twice, in two different locations."

"I'm up." Padded footsteps signaled her approaching the door. A sleepy Pressley swung it open. "What happened?"

"He struck again. How soon can you be ready?"

"Give me five minutes." She raced for the bathroom.

It took her seven. Jackson stopped his pacing when she rushed into the living room, the laptop bag she never went anywhere without clutched in one hand. She looked great in faded jeans and a tee shirt that looked like it should have been thrown away years ago. Her ponytail swung back and forth like a pendulum.

She followed his gaze. "Sorry. I slept in it and just pulled on some jeans."

"Gun?"

"In my bag."

"You stay by my side every second." He gave her a hard stare. "I mean it. No negotiations."

"Not a problem." She followed him to his car. "I'm aware of the danger."

Good. She needed to stay hypervigilant until Frank was behind bars.

Jackson put a revolving light on top of his car and sped toward the second crime scene. The victims of the first had survived, although one was wounded. Their next destination would be the hospital. En route, he explained what the chief had told him over the phone.

"Two?" Pressley's eyes widened.

"Yeah. Guess he messed up the first one." Jackson itched to get the man in his sights and pull the trigger.

"The original phantom didn't kill as often."

"Frank has a taste for it, obviously." He parked by the chief's car behind an abandoned warehouse. "He isn't sticking to the woods anymore. Instead, he seems to be seizing the opportunity when it presents itself." Jackson shoved open his car door and waited for Pressley to exit.

She followed him to where the chief stood next to a battered Impala. Inside a young African American couple had been shot and left in the front seat. No games this time, just the need to kill.

"I want this man found and stopped, Hudson." The chief shook his head. "The first night of a mandatory curfew, and he attacked two couples. I've called in reinforcements. They should arrive in a few hours. Miss Taylor, I'd like you to provide copies of all the information you've gathered."

"Yes, sir. I'll have them to you as soon as the photo shop opens."

"No, you'll bring them to the station when we're finished here. We can make copies." He marched to his squad car, leaving the scene for Jackson to handle.

Jackson turned to face the arriving reporters. "Stay here, Pressley. I'd prefer they not get you on camera. Stay down." Nodding, she sat on the ground in front of the victim's car, her gun clutched in her hand. She was wise to use the car as cover.

Jackson retrieved crime scene tape from the trunk of his car and secured the area, keeping the reporters back. That didn't stop them from speculating or shouting questions.

"Phantom Number Two is on a spree," one said. "What can you tell us?"

"Is this the work of one man or multiple killers?"

"Officer, who is behind the car? Is it a witness?"

"I've nothing to say at this point." Jackson finished taping off the area. "Chief Larson will do a press briefing later today." Cameras flashed. What a circus. Jackson groaned and waited for the EMTs and crime scene techs to arrive. While he waited, he shined the flashlight around the car, looking for a sign, any sign but found nothing. Concrete didn't allow for footprints. "You all right?" He stood next to where Pressley sat.

"Ground's a bit hard, but I'm okay." She shifted her position. "We can't allow him to keep killing, Jackson."

"I'm open to suggestions. Frank is as elusive as his relative was."

"You're going to have to let him come for me."

"I'm not going to use you as bait. Besides, once folks take the curfew seriously, he'll be attacking people in their homes. We have no way of stopping him. The city is too large." Hopefully, enough help would arrive to crowd the nighttime hours with cops. "Frank has dived off the deep end. All we can do is wait for him to make a mistake."

That wasn't going to happen in time to stop him from killing again.

Headlights flared to life through the trees. A second later, Jackson sprinted in that direction. They'd been watched the whole time.

~

Frank laughed as Hudson raced in his direction as if he could catch him on foot. What a fool. He spun the car around and sped in the opposite direction. He hadn't had this much fun in his entire life.

He'd sat there and watched as Pressley took a seat on the hard ground and Hudson taped off the area. He'd watched as the reporters shouted questions and snapped photos, not worried that they'd catch him in one of the pictures. No, he was far too good to be caught. His laughter increased as Hudson grew smaller and smaller in Frank's rearview mirror. All that could be seen was the tiny beam of light from the officer's flashlight.

What he wanted to do was grab Pressley. Instead, he made haste for the cabin he now called home. He'd get an opportunity to take her. Frank knew how people's minds worked. She'd tire of the killings, get careless, and make herself a target. It's what good people did. That's why those types were picked off by stronger ones like himself.

All he had to do was wait, and Frank Beckett was a patient man when he wanted something bad enough.

~

The police station swarmed with officers arriving from other cities in Arkansas. Pressley handed the Jump drive containing her notes to the receptionist. "I'd like the originals back, please. Chief Larson said to make copies."

"I'll have them back to you in a few minutes."

While she waited, the newly arrived officers asked Pressley how she identified The Phantom as Roy Beckett and why she and Jackson suspected Frank.

"I don't believe in coincidences, gentlemen, and Frank's disappearance when the killings started would be a big one."

Heads nodded. One officer from Little Rock asked, "What's the plan now? Are we to follow your lead or follow protocol?"

Pressley glanced at the chief. "Since I'm only a civilian studying the case from 1946, you should take your orders from Chief Larson."

"Agreed." The chief nodded. "The FBI will be arriving sometime today and will take over when they do. For now, I intend for each and every one of you to be pounding the pavements, starting just before curfew. If anyone is out without a darn good reason, issue a citation. This is to be given the utmost priority. My receptionist will be handing each of you the notes Miss Taylor has compiled. While our present killer has deviated from The Phantom's MO, there might be something in there to help us apprehend this guy."

More heads nodded before Chief Larson told Jackson he could take Pressley home.

"Are we really returning to your house?" She asked once they were outside.

"Just for a few hours to catch a few hours of sleep. Then, we need to come up with a plan because I don't have one." He exhaled heavily. "Other than visiting the hospital and possibly driving the streets tonight anyway."

After a short four hours of sleep, Jackson woke Pressley again, and they drove to the hospital to speak with last night's survivors. A nurse showed them to a hospital room where a sleeping young man lay on the bed, and a girl about his age sat in the chair beside him holding his hand.

"I'm Officer Hudson, and this is Miss Taylor. Do you mind answering a few questions for us?"

She glanced up with red-rimmed eyes. "We already told the police everything."

"Please." Pressley smiled, doing her best to reassure the girl. "I've been studying the case from 1946 and am hoping you can help us with this new one."

The girl sighed. "I'll try."

"Start with telling us what happened," Jackson said.

"We were sitting by the lake. Troy had asked me on a date, but neither one of us has much money. I didn't mind. I thought sitting on a blanket by the lake was a romantic idea. We hadn't been there long before a man in a ski mask showed up and told us to take off our clothes. We ran instead. When we reached the road, he shot Troy in the back. That's it." Her words broke on a sob. "The doctor said Troy might never walk again. Only time and physical therapy will tell."

Pressley placed a hand on the girl's shoulder. "That is unbelievably sad, but at least he's alive. Others weren't as lucky."

"Tell that to the star quarterback."

"Did you see what kind of car the man drove?"

"A dark sedan, I think. I couldn't see it well because of the trees. The man was dressed in jeans, a long-sleeved shirt, and the mask."

Not much more information than they had before.

"He said he wanted to have fun with me," she said softly as they turned to leave.

Thankfully, he hadn't had the chance. "Thank you." Pressley gave her shoulder a gentle squeeze. "We'll pray for Troy."

"Now what?" she asked in the hospital elevator. "A ski mask and jeans aren't much to go on."

"We know who the killer is." Jackson pressed the button for the bottom floor. "He also drives a dark sedan. Finding him is going to be the hard part. He strikes at night in remote places. The police can't cover every square inch of the city and the surrounding farmland. It's going to take a lot of luck."

She still thought the only way they'd catch Frank was to make it easy for him to get close to her. The difficult part would be convincing Jackson. Broken sleep and not enough of it made her brain fuzzy. "I need something to eat and at least two cups of coffee."

"There's a great burger place not too far from here. They claim to have the world's best coffee, but that's debatable."

The elevator doors opened, and they stepped into the lobby. "Sounds perfect if we're going to be up all night."

"It's time to switch our days and nights. We won't catch Frank during daylight."

She agreed. Evil liked the dark, slinking around searching for prey.

At a diner resembling a throwback to the 1950s, she chose a bacon cheeseburger, fries, and coffee with cream. While they waited for their food, she studied Jackson who seemed lost in his thoughts, staring at the diner's entrance.

"I had someone check on Frank's financials," he said. "He took money from the bank and visited the grocery store the day he disappeared."

"Stocking up on supplies so he need only come to town to kill."

"I've asked the chief to send a helicopter to scope out cabins in the outlying areas. He's going to speak with the FBI when they arrive." He faced her. "If they see any cabins not known to have been previously occupied, I'm willing to take the risk of you and me checking them out. Are you willing? This visit to Texarkana might be your last."

"I know." Not what she'd thought of when she arrived, but things had turned and made danger, even death, a grave possibility. "I'll risk almost anything to stop Frank Beckett."

"That's what I'm afraid of," Jackson muttered.

Chapter Thirteen

"These cops stick out like party dresses at a barn raising." Jackson leaned forward and glared through the windshield. "Frank won't move into the open with the police strolling down the sidewalk." What happened to blending in?

"There isn't usually this many people moving around. Especially during a curfew." Pressley slouched in her seat. What a waste of time.

The car radio crackled. Jackson snatched it from its holder. "Officer Hudson."

"We have a report of a woman saying she's spotted the man we're looking for outside her house." She gave the address.

Immediately, two officers sprinted in that direction. Jackson sighed and pulled the car away from the curb.

"Wouldn't we be more effective outside rather than sitting in the car?" Pressley tilted her head.

"You're safer in the car."

"Sure I am. Just as the other victims were." Frank was out there—she felt it deep down—crouched like a cougar ready to pounce. With too many obvious officers on the streets, he'd go outside of town or target someone on the outskirts.

Had Grandma felt the same frustration and anticipation all those years ago that Pressley felt now? The helplessness in bringing down a killer? Sure, Pressley had helped identify The Phantom, but now a more evil man stalked the town. She wasn't sure she could help stop him. Not sitting safely in a car anyway.

They pulled up to the address given, and surprise, surprise, Jackson allowed Pressley to join him outside the car. "Stay with me."

The man was startimg to sound like a broken record. "I know the drill."

He cut her a sharp glance, then joined the two officers in front of a two-story white house.

"False alarm," one of them said. "Nothing more than a raccoon digging in the garbage can."

"I really thought I saw someone lurking in the bushes." The woman pulled her fuzzy robe up around her neck. "A woman can't be too careful. My grandmother told me all about The Phantom, you know. The town even holds a party at Halloween."

Halloween came early this year. Pressley turned and surveyed the quiet suburban street. A few lights flicked on, curtains twitched as those inside watched the action outside. All seemed quiet. "Wait." She narrowed her eyes as a man in a mask slipped through a gate across the street. "Jackson." She took off at a run.

"Pressley!" Jackson caught up and gripped her arm. "Do you have a death wish?" He scowled and shoved her behind him.

Rolling her eyes, she followed him in the direction the man had gone. Catching sight of him scaling a fence,

Jackson aimed his gun. "Halt. Police."

The man froze and jumped to the ground, hands above his head. "Don't shoot. I'm just here to see my girlfriend."

"Remove your mask."

The man pulled off the ski mask revealing a face barely old enough to shave.

"Why the mask, son?" Jackson lowered his weapon. "Are you aware there's a killer who wears one?"

His mouth opened and closed a few times before he spoke. "I didn't want her parents to recognize me. They don't like me."

"Hiding behind a mask when the town is running scared could get you shot. You're breaking curfew." Jackson motioned for the young man to follow him, then turned him over to another officer. "Of all the idiotic things to do."

"It was stupid," Pressley said, "but young people don't always think before acting. You were young once."

"I followed the rules."

No argument there. She doubted Jackson ever got into trouble. Pressley, on the other hand, had always skirted the line and spent more time grounded during her senior year than not.

Gunshots sounded from a street over. Jackson, Pressley, and the officer not putting the kid in the squad car took off at a sprint. They arrived to see an old man on his porch with a shotgun.

"Thought I saw something," he said when they arrived.

"Give me that." Jackson yanked the weapon from the man's hands. "You could shoot an innocent person. The whole town has gone mad. Search the area," he told the other officer.

"I have the right to protect myself." The older man crossed his arms.

"Yes, sir, you do, but in a responsible manner." Jackson leaned the shotgun against the wall of the house. "There are officers patrolling the streets. You might shoot one of them."

Or a kid out breaking the rules. Pressley glanced around the manicured lawn. Not many places to hide. What had the man thought he saw? Whatever it was, if there had been something, it was long gone.

A squad car drove past, the officer speaking into a megaphone that curfew was in place and for folks to stay in their homes. Pressley shrugged. There would always be those who thought they knew more than the authorities and thought they could catch a killer when the police couldn't.

They returned to the car. "How about a drive to some houses outside of town?" Jackson asked. "I doubt Frank is anywhere near. There's too much going on."

"Sounds good." She clicked her seatbelt into place. While there would be patrols on the more remote roads, there wouldn't be as many, which made hiding easier.

A moonless night with a cloudy sky cast the country roads with eeriness. Swaying tree branches whispered of horror.

Pressley shook off her maudlin thoughts and kept her eyes peeled through the open car window. Where are you, Frank?

~

Frank stared through the window where a man and a woman watched TV, the changing colors on the screen flickering across their faces. He smiled, remembering a scene the newspapers had mentioned, back when Roy had all the fun.

He wished it was Hudson and Pressley sitting in the easy chair and flowered sofa. Yes, the woman had moved in with the cop. For her protection, no doubt. It didn't matter. Frank could still get to her when he was ready. For now, he was having too much fun to end it all.

Rapping the barrel of the pistol on the window, he laughed at the fear on the couple's faces when they spotted him. The woman screamed and darted down the hallway. Her husband snatched a handgun from an end table. Too slow. Frank's bullet caught him in the chest.

Frank moved to the door, only to find it locked. Not a problem considering the back door slammed against the house. The woman wanted a game of chase. Frank grinned, happy to oblige.

She stood in the center of the yard, a rifle aimed at him as he came around the corner. Clever. This one wanted to fight back. He admired her spunk and ducked back out of sight.

Her voice reached him. "The killer is at my house. He shot my husband. I'm armed, so have any arriving officers announce themselves."

She'd called the police. This could complicate things.

When he peered around the corner, he got a face full of wood splinters as her shot hit the corner of the house. He cursed and fired wildly. When he chanced a peek again, she'd taken shelter behind a large oak tree.

The inky blackness of the night made vision difficult. The woman knew her yard. Frank didn't. What if she snuck up behind him? He plastered his back against the siding. Stay or leave? He'd already killed the man. No one could survive a direct hit like that. Was staying around for the woman worth taking the risk of being shot himself?

Sirens wailed, halting in front of the house. How did they get there so fast? Frank eyed the cornfield in front of him. He'd have to make a run for it. Pushing away from the house, he stayed as low as possible and ran.

~

Gun in hand, Pressley right behind him, Jackson dashed around the house. "Police!"

A woman armed with a rifle pointed toward the cornfield. "He went in there. Is the ambulance coming?"

"Yes, ma'am. Stay out of sight." He turned to Pressley. "I'd like it if you stayed with her. Please."

She blinked up at him, then nodded. "Be careful. You should wait for backup."

"He'll get away. Call the station and let them know where I am." Jackson cupped her cheek and headed into the cornfield, praying Frank wouldn't double back and find Pressley. He stopped and listened, hearing nothing but the wind through the stalks. The man could be anywhere.

The back of his neck prickled. The palm of his hand holding the gun grew sweaty. A footfall sounded a few rows over. Staying low, Jackson headed that way, careful to make as little noise as possible. He wanted to call out, tell Frank he couldn't escape, but that would alert him to the fact it was Jackson chasing him. Which meant Pressley wouldn't be far. Jackson couldn't risk her safety to pinpoint Frank's location. The chance of catching him was slim.

A wild shot whipped through a stalk a few feet from Jackson. It came from his left so he headed in that direction. Jackson cringed as the radio on his belt crackled. He quickly pressed the off button.

Another shot, closer this time, had Jackson diving to the ground. He waited a few seconds before scrambling to his feet and moving forward.

Frank would have a car waiting somewhere close. He had to find him before he reached his vehicle. The odds were not in Jackson's favor.

The wind stopped, making moving through the cornfield more difficult as any movement would cause the stalks to sway and give away his position. He shook his head at his dumb luck and pressed on.

Sirens from the house meant the ambulance had arrived. *Please stay at the house, Pressley.* He wouldn't put it past her to follow him. He also didn't like her at the house alone, assuming the victim's wife went to the hospital. The woman had shown a strong backbone, and with Pressley, she could hopefully hold off Frank.

Jackson couldn't worry about that now. He needed to find the man and stop the deaths.

A car engine roared to life, spurring Jackson to a run. He left the field in time to see the taillights of a dark sedan speeding away. Jackson took aim and pulled the trigger, shooting out the back window. The second shot flattened a tire but didn't stop the car. It swerved and kept going, sending a hubcap into a nearby ditch. Frank Beckett had done it. Again.

Nothing to do but turn back. Jackson headed for the house and opened the back door. "Pressley?"

When no answer came, he searched the rooms only to find the house empty. "Pressley!" An icy fist gripped his heart. Why couldn't she follow his orders?

"I'm here." She stood in the back doorway.

Jackson rushed to her, pulling her into his arms. "Why did you go outside?"

"To wait for you." Her voice muffled against his chest. "I heard gunshots and feared the worst." She peered up at him. "Did you find him?"

"No. He drove away." He held her tighter, breathing in the scent of her fruit-fragrant shampoo. "I was afraid he'd double back and hurt you."

"I wouldn't have made it easy for him." She smiled. "I would have shot him, or tried to. I just want this all to end."

He sighed, praying she could pull the trigger if she had to. "Me too, sweetheart. Me too." He ran his hands down her arms, then took one of her hands in his. "Let's go home. We'll repeat this all again tomorrow night. One of these nights, we'll get lucky."

"Frank seems to be re-creating the news reports from Roy's spree. Except, Roy's ended after shooting the couple in a farmhouse. I don't think Frank's will."

He agreed. Frank wouldn't stop until he was dead or behind bars.

Chapter Fourteen

Stupid cop. He'd ruined everything. How had Hudson and Pressley known Frank was at the farmhouse? Coincidence? Maybe. Next time, he wouldn't be so careless.

Fighting the urge to kill again, he sped up the mountain to his temporary home. Temporary, because once he took care of Pressley, it was time to move to new territory. Somewhere outside of Arkansas.

His fingers drummed to the beat of the song on the radio as he tried to figure out how to get close to Pressley. It wouldn't be easy. Hudson never left her alone. There had to be a way to draw the officer away from her. Frank was a smart man. He'd think of something.

A deer darted from the woods. Frank cursed and yanked the wheel, sending the car barreling toward a tree. He yanked the wheel again. Instead of hitting the tree head on, he smashed the passenger side against the trunk. Air bags exploded.

His curses increasing, he fought to free himself of the seatbelt, opened his car door, and tumbled to the ground. To think he'd almost met his end by a deer.

Now what? He couldn't very well call a tow truck.

Frank reached into the car, snatched his gun from where it had fallen on the floorboard, and hiked to the cabin. Somehow, he'd have to find another vehicle, and soon.

He wasn't sure how long he walked before spotting a house set off in a field. No lights shone in the windows, but the fact cows slept in a meadow confirmed that the house was occupied. And living this far from town, there would definitely be a vehicle.

The back door gave a slight squeak when he pushed it open. Obviously, the occupants didn't expect anyone way out here and didn't lock their doors. Frank grinned. They made it easy for him. He stepped into a small kitchen and listened.

No barking, no cry of alarm. He pulled a small flashlight from his pocket and moved to the next room, rolling his shoulders. Dang, those airbags hurt when they deployed. He'd feel sore for a few days. A set of car keys rested on a small table near the front door. Frank pocketed them and glanced down the small hallway. Should he risk killing the home's occupants or leave while the going was good?

He took the safe path and left the house the same way he'd come. Frank found a car and a small pickup in a makeshift carport. The keys fit the truck. Two minutes later, Frank drove slowly away from the house.

~

"Pressley?" Jackson knocked on her bedroom door.

"Go away." She pulled the blankets over her head.

"We have to check on a stolen vehicle. The chief doesn't want to pull any of the other officers off finding Frank."

She kicked the sheet off her legs. "I thought that's what we were doing." Lack of sleep always made her cranky. Today was no exception. "I'm coming."

It wasn't a surprise that Chief Larson would send Jackson on less important items. His main objective was to keep her safe until Frank came for her. But how could they do both? Help find Frank and serve the community before they collapsed from exhaustion?

She plodded to the bathroom and splashed cold water on her face, washing the grit from her eyes. Dark circles shadowed them. With a sigh, she changed into jeans and a tee-shirt, her normal attire it seemed. Pressley would love to dress pretty again, see a spark of admiration in Jackson's eyes, but chasing a killer and visiting crime scenes didn't call for a dress and heels.

The aroma of brewing coffee greeted her as she headed for the kitchen. "Bless you." She gratefully accepted the travel cup Jackson held out to her.

"We'll pick up breakfast on the way," he said. "You okay?"

"Just sleep-deprived. The coffee will help."

Jackson led the way to his car and headed up the mountain. They spent a lot of time in his car. More than at his house, it seemed.

When would life go back to normal? But that would mean it was time for her to go home. Pressley cut Jackson a sideways glance. What if she didn't want to walk away from this man? She'd never met one so honest, kind, and upright. She was smart enough to recognize a gem when she saw one.

Pressley groaned inwardly. Jackson might call her sweetheart, but maybe he did that to all the women in his life. It didn't mean he wanted a relationship with her. She was nothing more than a job to him. The thought sent a pang through her heart. The coffee offered no distraction from the pang. Now, she was not only tired but depressed. What she needed was a good, solid night's sleep.

Jackson sent a worried look her way. "Are you sure it's only tiredness?"

"Yes." She forced a smile. "Maybe we can squeeze in a nap before hitting the streets again tonight."

He reached over and gave her hand a gentle squeeze. "I'll make sure of it."

There he went, being kind again despite her grumpiness. She rested her head against the seat back and released a long exhale. *Show yourself, Frank. I'm tired.*

Jackson passed a car on the side of the road, then backed up. "That looks like Frank's car."

She turned her head. "He isn't the only person who drives a dark sedan."

Shoving his door open, he stepped out of the car. "I agree, but it's worth taking a look. You can stay there."

"No, thanks." She followed him, circling the car, noting the skid marks on the road. "What do you think happened?"

"Looks like the driver swerved to avoid hitting something and lost control. My guess is a deer. Accidents happen a lot on these country roads." Jackson climbed through the driver's door and shoved aside the air bags to open the glove compartment. He held up a slip of paper. "Registered to Frank Beckett."

~

Had Frank been heading home or searching for his next victims? Since a truck had just been reported stolen and no one was killed at the home of the owner, he must have been headed to his hideout. The mountain they were on wasn't large, but it was heavily wooded. Maybe they'd just run across their first piece of luck.

He radioed for a tow truck and also asked for a helicopter, then he turned back to Pressley. "I'd like to search the immediate area before heading to the house of the stolen truck."

"Okay. There's a slim chance Frank might be lying wounded somewhere, right?"

"If we could only be so lucky."

After half an hour of searching, Jackson determined Frank had gone ahead on foot. He'd bet his favorite boots the truck had been stolen by the very man they sought. A few minutes later, they arrived at the house of the stolen vehicle.

A man, armed with a rifle, stepped onto the porch as Jackson and Pressley climbed out of the car. Jackson retrieved a fingerprint kit from the trunk. "I'm Officer Hudson. This is Pressley Taylor. We're here about the stolen vehicle."

"Glad to meet you. I'm Harvey Olson. My wife is Hazel. Come on in." He stepped back and held the door open. "We never lock our doors. That's how the thief must have gotten in. We won't make that mistake again."

"If the thief is who we think it is, you're lucky to be alive, Mr. Olson." Jackson pulled a small notepad from his jacket pocket. "Can you describe the vehicle that was taken?"

"A dark green Ford 150. Had my hunting rifle hanging in the window. The thief took the keys right off that table." He pointed to a glass dish that held another set of keys. "Best I figure, he came through the back door. The missus locked the front. Said she felt like she needed to. I wish she would've locked the back."

"Probably wouldn't have made a difference. Mind if I check the back door?"

"Go ahead. Nothing to see, though." Mr. Olson stepped aside to let Jackson pass.

Jackson dusted the door handles and frame, then used tape to lift the print. If the prints didn't prove to be Frank's, he'd be surprised. He turned and walked from the kitchen, stopping right outside the door and glanced down a short hall. "Where were you sleeping?"

"First room on the right."

The Olsons were very lucky indeed. "Where is your wife now?"

"She went to town for groceries. I don't want her to know this killer roaming the countryside might be the thief. It would give her a heart attack."

"No need to frighten her unnecessarily. Make sure to lock your doors and keep your gun handy. Where did you keep the truck?"

"Follow me." He led them to a double carport. "Had it parked right here. The scoundrel drove off bold as brass. Good thing I have insurance. I'll get it replaced, but I loved that hunting rifle."

"Sorry for the loss." Jackson understood. He had a fondness for his handgun, something a law enforcement officer was rarely without. "We'll let you know if we find your truck." He motioned his head for the silent Pressley to follow him back to the car.

"Frank could have killed them." She turned to face Jackson. "Why didn't he?"

"Maybe he's injured and thought holing up for a while the better choice." They could hope for that at least. It would mean no murders for a few days.

She glanced down the road. "He's here, somewhere

close. I feel it."

Jackson glanced up to see a helicopter fly over. Good. They'd listened this time. "The pilot will make note of every building he spots. Frank has to be in one of them. We'll check them all."

What would she do once Frank was caught? Pressley had come to town to find out the identity of The Phantom. She'd done that. Now, she was helping to catch Frank, relying mostly on her instincts, which were good if not better than Jackson's. Then, she'd leave. The thought punched Jackson in the gut. Would she stay if he asked her? What a ridiculous question. "What job did you leave to come here?"

She laughed. "After caring for my grandmother for the last couple of years, I thought about writing a book. That's the second reason for coming here. I still plan on writing the true account of The Phantom. Grandma left me enough to live on for a couple of years. After that—" she shrugged. "I'll figure it out. I've always wanted to be an author. Now I have the opportunity."

That brightened his spirits a bit. She could write anywhere. Maybe she'd stay in Texarkana if he asked her to. But first, they had to catch a killer without becoming victims.

He sent her a smile. "Let's head to the station, fill out the theft report, then head home for a few hours of shut-eye. How does that sound?"

"Like heaven." She grinned. "Hopefully, tonight's driving around will be a waste of time."

No time spent with her would be a waste.

Chapter Fifteen

After a week of no deaths and no sighting of Frank, local law enforcement decided he'd crawled off to die after his crash on the lonely road. Pressley knew better. Evil only waited for its chance to strike again.

Life in Texarkana returned to normal. The curfew was lifted, and the teenagers started hanging out again. Pressley shook her head and let the curtain on Jackson's window fall into place.

With the danger seemingly gone, she had no more reason to stay in town except for the man sipping coffee at the kitchen table. He hadn't asked her to leave, didn't seem to resent her being in his house. In fact, they'd settled into a routine of sorts. He'd go to work, and she'd follow and write on her book at whatever desk was empty at the moment.

"What's wrong?" He glanced up from his coffee.

"Nothing."

He chuckled. "Even I know when a woman says nothing, she means something. Sit, sweetheart. Tell me what's on your mind?"

She poured her second cup of coffee of the morning and joined him at the table. "Do you think Frank is dead or moved on?"

"Nope." He put a hand on hers. "He'll show his ugly face again."

"I feel as if I'm spinning my wheels here." She swallowed past the burn in her throat.

"Why?" His brow furrowed. "You said there's nothing for you at home."

"I came to fulfill my grandmother's wish, and I have."

"So? Stay. I've plenty of room. No need to be in a hurry to go."

She studied his face. Did he actually want her to stay? Why didn't he ask? The warm look in his eyes gave her hope, but she wanted to hear the words from his lips.

"The FBI agents are leaving today. The reporters have already gone." She returned her attention to the cup in her hand. "That leaves us with limited resources if Frank returns."

"See? You're needed here."

"For how long?"

"For as long as it takes. He'll either show his face again or we'll find his body. I'm hoping for the latter." He rose and rinsed out his cup. "Ready to head to the station?"

"Yes." She took another sip and rinsed her own cup before retrieving her bag from her room.

The day consisted of mundane calls about vandalism, disturbing the peace, and Pressley writing while Jackson filled out reports. Going along with him on his rides helped break up the morning and kept boredom at bay. Still, her nerves stretched tight, waiting for news of another murder and praying one never came.

"Ready for lunch?"

She glanced up from her laptop to see Jackson standing over her. "Sure." She packed the computer and followed him outside. "What do you feel like?"

"Tacos." He grinned. "I know the perfect place. We can purchase them and eat by the lake if you'd like."

"Sounds great." She hoped they had fish tacos.

Jackson purchased chicken for himself and fish for her from a trailer with outside seating. Food in hand, he drove them to the lake.

Pressley couldn't help but remember the last time she'd been there with him, at night, after one of Frank's murder attempts. She was definitely glad it was daytime.

The sun sparkled on the water as she helped Jackson spread an old blanket on the ground. After they sat, he handed out their lunch and drinks. "Nothing like a day by the water," he said.

She nodded. "Except for nighttime when the moon leaves a trail of silver." What was she doing? That sounded like an invitation for him to bring her at night. "I bet you brought plenty of girls here when you were in high school."

"Not so many, but there was one that I really liked. We mostly went to Lovers' Lane, back when it was safe to go parking."

"It'll be safe again. What happened to her?"

He shrugged. "We went to different colleges and drifted apart. What about you? Ever had a special guy in your life?"

"Once, but he wasn't thrilled with the amount of time I spent looking after my grandmother. She took priority in my life for a few years. His leaving showed me he wasn't the one for me."

"Idiot." Jackson smiled and bit into his taco. Sauce

ran down his chin.

Before she could think better of it, she reached over and wiped his face with her napkin.

His gaze softened as he leaned forward and kissed her, softly at first, then cupping the back of her head to bring her closer. He tasted slightly of chicken spices. She closed her eyes and gave in, returning his kiss with the emotions rising within her. Again, she mentally coaxed him to ask her to stay.

"I like kissing you," he murmured before pulling away. He gave her a wink and returned to his food.

Good. She liked kissing him, too. She smiled and finished her food, then rested back on her elbows to watch a pair of mallard ducks swim nearby. Since Jackson hadn't asked her to leave, she'd stay a while longer. Pressley still hadn't decided what to do with the house Grandma left her. There was no hurry.

They returned a few minutes later to the station, Jackson to his desk, Pressley to her book. Same old routine that now felt as comfortable as her favorite sweatpants. She angled so she could see Jackson every time she glanced up from her writing. Not only did she enjoy his kisses, but she liked looking at him when he didn't know it.

~

Frank watched through the truck windshield from the safety of some low-lying branches. Imagine his surprise and relief when he'd felt well enough to return to town and found the extra law enforcement gone. It hadn't taken the town long to return to their normal activities.

Young lovers strolled the sidewalk hand in hand. All he had to do was decide which ones to follow. He didn't care if they went home or somewhere else to park. Either way, he'd take care of the itch that had grown as he healed from his accident.

The day after he'd wrecked his car, he barely was able to move. Bruises from the seatbelt had colored his chest. Not only did he need to kill again, but he needed supplies, which would be more difficult. Frank shrugged. He'd rob a convenience store and take what he needed.

The police would know it was him, but he'd be long gone before they arrived. Maybe he could find his next victim where he bought his supplies, then he'd head back to the cabin before anyone could send out an alarm.

Decision made, he pulled from his hiding place and headed to a convenience store on the outskirts of town. That late at night only one other vehicle sat in front of the store. Frank pulled to the side of the building and donned his mask. Grabbing his gun, he exited the truck and marched inside the store.

The clerk and one other man were the only ones there. Frank had hoped for a woman but couldn't be choosy at this point. He quickly disposed of the two men and started gathering food and bottles of water into a handheld basket.

Frank was so busy gathering items, he forgot to be alert. He glanced up into the startled eyes of an older couple who hightailed it back to their car and sped away. He gritted his teeth, realizing he'd lost a prime chance to take out a man and a woman. Knowing they'd alert the police, he quickly grabbed the rest of what he needed and raced away from the store.

As he drove, it occurred to him that not only did he target couples, but Roy had, too. He knew why Roy did.

It had been a strange attempt to exact revenge on the woman who had dumped him. Why did Frank want a man and a woman? It was more than assaulting the woman. Was he that much like his great relative?

No. Frank was much smarter. He'd already surpassed Roy's record and was still going strong. The police were nowhere near putting a stop to his spree.

He laughed, temporarily satiated, and he headed back to his cabin home.

~

The ringing of his phone jolted Jackson from a deep sleep where he dreamed of more kisses from Pressley. "Hudson." They told him of a murder/robbery in a convenience store. Witnesses waited for him at the police station. "On my way." He rapped on Pressley's door and received a mumbled reply that she'd be ready in five minutes. Rushing back to his room, he quickly dressed and waited for her by the front door.

"Is it Frank?" She asked hurrying toward him.

"Murder and robbery is all I know. We'll speak to the witnesses first, then head to the location where the crime took place." He locked the door behind them and opened the passenger side for her before getting into the driver's seat.

He hadn't had time to wonder if it was Frank or not. Didn't sound like him, but Jackson wasn't ruling anything out. What a horrible end to what had been a wonderful day.

An older couple waited in the conference room. Jackson and Pressley sat across from them. "Can I get you coffee or water?" Jackson asked.

They both shook their heads. The man spoke, his visibly upset wife crying into a tissue.

"Please tell me what you saw." Jackson slid a box of Kleenex across the table.

"We're the Langleys, traveling through town. We stopped to buy a caffeinated drink so we could make it a little farther before finding a hotel. I saw the dead guy next to the counter first, then looked up to see a man in a ski mask filling a basket with food and water. When he looked up, we ran. That's it. We came straight here."

"That was the wisest choice you could have made." The two were very lucky. Whether the man was Frank or not, he'd already killed two people. He finished questioning the couple, then returned to the car with Pressley. With a sigh, he turned the key in the ignition and drove to the crime scene.

"Maybe it isn't him," Pressley said. "Nothing out of the ordinary has happened in a week."

"It sounds like him."

"Lots of thieves wear a ski mask. Too bad the couple hadn't got a glimpse of what the man drove."

"I'll have a good idea if tire tracks were left behind." He knew in his gut the man who shot the two others was Frank. Jackson parked in front of the store and held the crime scene tape up for Pressley to duck under, then approached the first responding officer. "What can you tell me?"

"Same caliber bullet as The Phantom 2 uses. One kill shot to each man. The clerk is behind the counter. Bags of chips on the floor say the suspect left in a hurry, grabbing what he could."

Jackson nodded. "He'd know the couple who fled would call the cops. Any other reports of shootings?"

"Not yet."

"Let's hope there aren't any." He motioned his head

toward the back door for Pressley to follow him.

"Neither Roy or Frank have targeted just men," she said, stepping outside. "An opportunity killing?"

"More than likely. He needed supplies. Shot the two in the store, took what he needed, and left." He shined his flashlight across the cracked asphalt.

Grass and weeds grew in sporadic clusters in the dirt covering the asphalt. Jackson shined his light's beam, searching for tracks. There. He squatted to get a better look. Not only tire tracks but size eleven shoes. The tire tracks would fit a Ford 150 truck. "It was Frank."

"He's back," Pressley whispered. "It's starting again."

Jackson nodded. One week's reprieve wasn't nearly enough, although the townsfolk had quickly let down their guard. "I'm afraid the killings might increase if he's changing his MO." They needed to find him and find him fast.

Chapter Sixteen

Frank stepped onto the sagging cabin porch to the sound of a helicopter circling overhead. He'd have to ditch the truck and run. Where would he be able to hide now? He should have killed the couple he'd stolen the truck from. Hudson might not have been able to find him as easily, not knowing what he drove.

He ducked back inside, shoved what supplies he could into a large backpack, then his few items of clothing into a duffel bag and made a run for the thick trees behind the cabin. Those in the helicopter might know he was on the mountain, but the foliage would hide him until he found a new place to hole up.

Maybe he'd throw everyone for a loop and stay with the group of homeless men and women on the outskirts of town. He could blend in easily enough, at least for a while, but he'd need a vehicle to get there. Hopefully, he'd run across another farm. If not, he'd improvise. Frank considered himself the king of improv.

Frank slapped a branch out of his face, cursing when it slapped him back. He put a hand to his cheek, seeing a trace of blood. Score one for nature.

The helicopter continued to circle the area, but he

was secure in the fact they wouldn't see him through the thick trees. Sure, a herd of law enforcement would converge on the cabin, but finding Frank would be a lot harder on foot.

~

Pressley had started packing her suitcase a few days ago and now unpacked. Her time in Texarkana wasn't finished.

"You were going to leave?" Jackson stood in the doorway, a pained look on his handsome face. "Without saying anything?"

"My time here was done. I wouldn't have left without saying goodbye."

He stared at her for a minute, then, his words clipped, informed her they had a lead on where Frank might be staying. Before she could respond, he whirled and marched away, leaving her with her heart at her feet.

She ran after him. "Jackson, stop, please." She put a hand on his arm. "If you want me to stay, all you have to do is ask." There, she'd thrown into the wind what she longed for him to say.

"I don't want you to do anything you don't want to." His features hardened.

"Is it so hard to ask?" She said softly. "This is your house, your town."

"Don't you like it here?"

"Yes." She inwardly begged him to answer the question. Why was it so hard for him to be vulnerable, even for a moment?

"Will you stay?" The look in his eyes seemed afraid of her answer. "I want you to stay."

She smiled. "Yes. I will. For as long as you want me."

He returned her smile and pulled her into a hug. "Now that's settled, we have work to do."

Just like that, her insecurities rose. She wanted to ask if he only needed her until Frank was caught. Instead, she nodded and retrieved her bag from the bed. "Let's go."

Jackson drove her to the airport. "Ever been in a helicopter?"

"No." She froze, not wanting to ride in one this time, either. "I'm afraid of heights."

"Are you afraid of flying?" He arched a brow.

"In something that size, yes. I prefer a big jet."

"I'll protect you." He grinned.

"You aren't the pilot. Can't we drive?"

"It would take too long." He took her hand and pulled her toward the machine.

She dragged her feet, prolonging the minutes until she had to climb in. Her breath came in pants. "Wait." She pulled her hand free and bent over, trying to breathe away the anxiety.

Jackson put a hand on her back. "I'll hold your hand the entire time. It'll be fine. I promise. Do you trust me?"

"With my life." She glanced up. "But I don't trust that thing." She pointed at the helicopter.

Laughing, he guided her inside and buckled her in before handing her headphones. Then, he climbed in the other side and told the pilot they were ready.

The copter lifted into the air, sending Pressley's stomach into her throat. She kept a death grip on Jackson's hand and her other on the strap hanging next to her head. The thump thump of the copter's blades drowned out all sound, reverberating in her chest. She closed her eyes and prayed.

"Relax, sweetheart. We'll be there in a few minutes." Jackson's voice came through her headset.

Easy for him to say. Every breeze seemed to cause the copter to shudder and shake, lift and drop. She was going to throw up. Pressley breathed through her mouth and counted to ten.

"We'll be landing in less than five minutes," the pilot said. "There's a crosswind, so landing will be rough."

Just what she needed. She squeezed her eyes tighter.

When they landed, she undid her seatbelt and scrambled out. "Can we have a car pick us up?"

"Sure." Jackson grinned. "Let's see what we can find out about our elusive killer."

She turned to study a ramshackle cabin, the front door hanging open, the stolen truck parked out front. The pilot of the copter was good. The clearing was barely big enough to land. As the copter rose back into the air, kicking up dirt, Pressley's hair pulled from her ponytail holder and whipped around her head. Her breathing finally returned to normal after having survived the scariest thing she'd ever endured.

Two police officers exited the cabin. "About time you arrived, Hudson," one said. "We've been here half an hour. The place is empty. Looks like the perp left in a hurry. Didn't take everything, just what he could carry on foot."

Pressley glanced toward the thick woods behind the cabin. *Where are you going, Frank? Where will you hide this time?* She turned and followed Jackson into the cabin.

~

Jackson could hardly believe Frank had actually

lived in such a rundown place. Sunlight squeezed through cracks in the plank walls. Dust covered whatever surfaces he hadn't used. No indoor plumbing or bathroom. Where had the man showered? With everyone in town on the lookout, even going to the gym would be almost impossible.

He moved back outside and headed for the woods at the rear of the cabin. Size eleven footprints here and there. From the spacing, he could tell Frank had run. Most likely upon seeing the circling copter. Shaking his head, he pounded his thigh, then returned to where Pressley waited. "We'll never find him in there."

"What's our next move?" Concern crossed her pretty face.

"We keep looking. He's up here somewhere, unless he stole another vehicle." Jackson didn't think he'd leave the owners alive this time. The next time they heard of Frank, more people would be dead. The man was a killing machine. "The chief will have to implement a curfew again."

"Will you call for a car?" She asked again, her eyes imploring him to say yes.

"Yes, but it will take a while. Might as well make yourself comfortable."

"We have one on the way," one of the officers said. "Instead of coming back for us, we thought it best the copter keep searching the mountain."

"Excellent." Although he wouldn't find anything useful, Jackson returned to the cabin and searched the two rooms. A few articles of clothing, some food and water, and nothing else but rodent poop, cobwebs, and dust.

Back outside, he glanced again at the woods, then

sat on the porch steps next to Pressley to wait for their ride. He entwined his fingers with hers, glad she'd decided to stay. When he'd seen her suitcase, his heart had stopped, letting him know how much he wanted her by his side. Jackson didn't know whether she'd stay after they caught Frank, but he'd do everything in his power to make her want to remain. Her leaving was not something he wanted to live through.

A van pulled in front of them. Time to go. *Go where* was the question. Frank wouldn't strike during the daylight. When he did, they wouldn't know anything until after the fact. He and Pressley might as well head back to the precinct.

When they arrived, the rest of the day settled into their routine. Things were calm in town, allowing Jackson to catch up on reports. He'd glance up once in a while to watch Pressley typing on her laptop, her hair secured once again in its ponytail. He smiled, preferring it whipping around her face.

She looked up, her blue eyes fixed on him. Her lips curled into a smile before she returned her attention to her writing.

"How's the book coming?" he asked, reluctant to let her attention drift away from him.

"Good, although we don't yet know the ending, do we?" She kept typing. "But we will. I know it in my gut."

Hopefully, the ending didn't result in one of them dying. He lived with that threat every day, but Pressley shouldn't have to. The longer the killings went on, the harder it would be for Jackson to keep her safe.

Yes, the chief had assigned her to Jackson not only to locate Frank, but to keep her from being killed. He prayed he was up to the task.

"You look worried." Pressley's gaze fixed on him. "Need a break?"

"From all this?" He waved his arm. "I don't see that happening anytime soon."

"Neither do I." She gave a sad smile and returned to her work.

Jackson plucked a pencil from a nearby cup and tapped it on his desk pad. They needed a break in the case.

Frank had disappeared, similar to Roy's disappearance back in 1946, except Roy had been institutionalized. His great nephew wouldn't suffer the same fate. He'd show his ugly head again, and more people would die. Where would he hide? Where could he hide?

He lunged to his feet, dropping the pencil on his desk, then grabbed Frank's photo from the case board. "I have an idea."

"Okay?" Pressley packed up her things. "Are you going to share your idea?"

"If someone wanted to hide, and their last place was located, where would they go?"

She shrugged and shook her head.

"In plain sight." Jackson grinned. "Where in town can someone seemingly disappear?"

"Again, I got nothing."

He slung an arm around her shoulders and led her from the building. "A place with lots of people who mostly go unnoticed."

She blinked a few times. "Where the homeless hang out?"

"Exactly. I want to show Frank's photo to the shelters, soup kitchens, and the edge of town where the homeless tend to stay."

"Good job." Her face lit up. "Smart thinking. No one would notice another homeless person."

"The soup kitchen might, but those living in the field wouldn't pay him any undue attention unless he caused problems." He opened the passenger side door of his car.

As they drove away from the station and approached the homeless shelter, Jackson studied every transient person they passed. One woman dug in the garbage outside a fast-food restaurant. A man slouched against the wall of a drugstore, a brown paper sack clutched in his hand.

Frank wouldn't be one of these. He hadn't reached the point of digging for food or hanging out in the open. No, he'd make sure to keep himself surrounded except for when he ventured out to find his next victims.

"Do you think the homeless will speak to you while you're in uniform?" Pressley's gaze locked on his.

"You're right. We'll need to head home to change." Jackson turned the car around. How could he not have realized his uniform would lock people's lips? Rookie mistake. He'd change, then start the questioning. Someone out there had to know something. They couldn't keep coming up against an impenetrable wall. Frank would have to make a mistake sooner or later.

Chapter Seventeen

Frank huddled under a tattered sleeping bag, unable to believe life had come to living among the homeless. The odor of their unwashed bodies and alcohol-infused breath made him want to gag.

He narrowed his eyes as a woman and child rushed past him. When they'd gone a few yards, he stuffed his belongings behind a dumpster and followed them, the weight of his handgun heavy in the pocket of his coat. Frank pulled on his ski mask and drew up the hoodie on the oversized sweatshirt he wore. Not even his mother would recognize him.

The couple continued to hurry through those propped against trees and cement walls. Ah, they were headed toward the soup kitchen. He'd have to hurry before they left the area. Frank increased his pace, darting to the left and circling around to block their path. He grinned beneath his mask at the look on the woman's face. She drew her child close to her side.

The boy stared up, wide-eyed at Frank as he raised his gun. Then of all things, his hand lowered. He couldn't shoot a child no matter how much the urge to kill gnawed at him. Frank shoved two one-hundred-dollar bills at the woman, then whirled and raced away.

~

Pressley followed Jackson inside the town's soup kitchen and studied the people in line and sitting at tables. "This is sad."

"I agree." Jackson followed her gaze. "America shouldn't have such a homeless problem. Let's see if we can find the director."

A woman and boy around the age of twelve rushed into the dining hall. "I saw him. The Phantom." She sagged into a chair amidst the rising voices around her.

Jackson switched directions. "Ma'am? I'm Officer Hudson." He sat across from her, Pressley taking the seat next to him. "Can you tell me exactly what happened?"

She dabbed her eyes with a napkin from a dispenser, and she nodded. "I've never been more frightened in my life. A big man wearing a ski mask pointed a gun at me and my son. He just stared at us for a couple of minutes, then shoved money into my hand and ran off." She tilted her head. "That doesn't sound like the man terrorizing this city, but I swear it was him."

Pressley widened her eyes. "Maybe he can't bring himself to kill a child."

"I guess even Frank has some scruples. Where did you see him, ma'am?"

"Where all the homeless are. We were headed here for supper when he stepped in front of us." She put her arm around her son. "Our situation is temporary."

Pressley sure hoped so. "Come on. Let's get you a plate." She led the boy away while Jackson continued to question his mother. "Looks like spaghetti tonight. Smells yummy."

The boy nodded.

"You're okay now, but I bet that man was scary."

Could the boy speak?

He simply nodded again and stood at the back of the line.

The queue moved quickly despite the number of people, and Pressley took a plate for the boy's mother. She couldn't imagine the anxiety of not having a place to live. Jackson's house might not be her home, but she was safe, warm, and well fed. Maybe serving sometime in the soup kitchen while she was in town would be a good thing for her.

Plates in hand, she led the boy back to his mother and set the plate on the table in front of the woman. "You must be starving."

"Thank you."

Jackson pushed to his feet. "I have enough information. Let's pay a visit to the lot where the homeless live. Ma'am, please use the money you were given to sleep under a roof tonight. The kitchen can direct you to a shelter for you and your boy. There's no need to sleep outside."

Tears sprang to her eyes. "Thank you. I'll check into it."

Once outside, Jackson turned to Pressley. "These types of situations rip at my heart. No one should be homeless, much less a child."

"I've decided I'd like to volunteer here."

He smiled. "How about we both do that on my days off?"

She hugged his arm. "Sounds wonderful." While she spent twenty-four seven with Jackson, she'd enjoy doing something other than watching him work across the desk or hitting the pavement looking for Frank. Serving together would be something a real couple did together.

Heads turned as they entered the part grass, part cement lot. A few trees provided shade during the daylight hours but not nearly enough. Summer days would be hot. She noted a water spigot near one of the buildings and turned the nozzle. Water rushed from the pipes. At least these people had water.

"An anonymous person keeps the water running. Unfortunately, the building is deemed inhabitable." Jackson pulled Frank's photo from his pocket.

Head after head shook as he showed the picture and described the clothes Frank wore.

"He'd be wearing a dark hoodie and, occasionally, a ski mask."

"In this heat?" A bearded man scowled. "He'd stand out like a star in the moonless sky, wouldn't he? Ain't seen anyone matching that description."

"He'd be new," Pressley added. "Just today or last night."

"Nope." He cradled an almost empty bottle of cheap wine to his chest. "Keep asking. You might get lucky."

They moved on, meeting the same response. How could Frank not stand out? He wouldn't indulge in liquor that would dull his senses. His clothes wouldn't show the same wear as the others did. Had these people really not seen him or were they simply not talking?

Jackson started to lose hope. Not wearing his uniform didn't seem to loosen any lips.

Then, "Yeah, I saw him." A man blinked up at them with blurry eyes. "You a cop?"

"Does it matter?" Jackson squared his shoulders.

"Nah. I ain't done nothing wrong."

"Mind telling me where you saw this man?" Did he

have to pull information out bit by bit?

"He was following some woman and her kid."

"Do you know where he's staked his sleeping spot?"

The man motioned further down the line of tents and boxes. "That way somewhere. Dude's creepy. Always whistling."

"Whistling?"

"Yeah. Sounds like a white-throated thrush."

If Jackson were Frank, he'd choose a place on the outskirts where he could make a run for it if he needed to. "Thanks." He turned to Pressley. "Keep your eyes peered. He could be anywhere."

"I feel bad for saying this, but this place gives me the creeps." She wrapped her arms around herself.

"I doubt they see a clean, pretty woman that smells good very often." He smiled.

"I smell good?"

"Like strawberries and cream." He loved the scent of her, the feel of her…he swallowed against a suddenly dry throat. Was he in love with Pressley Taylor? Probably, which meant it would be even harder for him to let her go if she decided to head back to Northern Arkansas.

He shook off the depressing thought of her leaving and turned his attention back to the matters at hand. No sense worrying about the future when they had something more pressing to deal with, like keeping Frank from getting his hands on Pressley or killing again.

A few more people admitted to seeing a newcomer among their midst, but most clammed up like a tight lid on a pickle jar. It didn't matter. They had enough witnesses to suggest Frank was somewhere close.

"We shouldn't have come empty-handed," Pressley

said. "We could have brought blankets, pillows, clothing—"

"You'd have been swarmed and wouldn't have brought enough anyway." He admired her kind heart, but her naiveté could get her hurt. "There's food at the kitchen, and those other things are handed out from the shelter. All they have to do is ask."

They continued on, asking questions, showing the photograph, and catching no sight of Frank. Either he'd moved on, gone into town to find his next victims, or watched them from some dark corner. Jackson didn't like any of those options.

"We might as well head back. At least we know he's around somewhere. Feel up to a drive around the outskirts?"

Pressley nodded. "It's late enough for him to scout out prey. Should we see if we can't find some teens parking and send them home? The curfew started, but not all of them will pay attention."

"It'll be like looking for that proverbial needle in a haystack, but it's a start." They returned to his car outside the kitchen, which had closed up for the night. "We can start at Lovers' Lane, but that isn't the only place the teens go."

"Any parties in town?"

He arched a brow. "What's your thought?"

"In my grandmother's notes, Roy had followed a young couple from a social gathering. It had been a small musical production and dance, but a party would be the same thing. Any parties might be breaking up about now."

"Sweetheart, you have quite the amazing brain." He turned the key in the ignition and headed for the high school as a start. If nothing was hopping around there, he'd head into the suburbs.

The school was dark and locked up tight, as was normal during the summer months. Any sports practices would have ended hours ago. Jackson headed for the nearest housing development, driving slow and watching for any signs of young people gathering.

He heard them before he saw them. In a cul-de-sac, a party was in full swing. He parked a little ways away. "We might as well break this party up. It's past curfew."

Pressley put a hand on his arm to stop him from getting out of the car. "Call another officer to break it up. We can't possibly follow them all home, and if we're out, Frank might spot us."

He sighed. "You're right. Which couple will we follow?" The whole thing was impossible. Frank might not even be close. There could be other parties, social events, dates at the theater—so many possibilities.

He radioed in the call, then waited, drumming his fingers on the steering wheel. This was the first case he'd ever had that made him feel helpless. Frank stayed one step ahead of them. Something had to give.

"We will catch him," Pressley said.

He nodded. Frank would kill again and again until law enforcement stopped him. All they had to go on right now was that he lived among the homeless and might be searching for his next victims at social gatherings. It was definitely not enough.

A few minutes later, lights flashing sans siren, a squad car pulled up to the party. A uniformed officer slid out and approached the house, tossing a wave over his shoulder to where Jackson and Pressley sat. After ringing the doorbell, he stepped back as the door opened and a young man's form was illuminated from the light inside. When he'd finished, the officer approached Jackson's car.

"They're going to break it up," Officer Mercer said.

"Can you park somewhere out of sight and follow a young couple as they leave? Maybe get some other officers to do the same? We'll follow a couple, too."

"You think The Phantom will strike?"

Jackson nodded. "If not here, somewhere, but we can't be everywhere."

The officer clapped his hand on the top of the car. "Will do. Stay safe."

"You, too."

A laughing couple who looked to be the age of recent graduates exited the gate to the backyard and climbed into a battered pickup. Jackson started his car and pulled out behind them as they drove away.

The truck turned into a gas station and the young man exited, marching straight to Jackson's vehicle. "Are you following us, man?" He crossed his arms.

Jackson showed his badge. "Yes, we are. Local law enforcement are trying to insure that you young people make it home all right. Are you headed straight home?"

"Yeah, I have work tomorrow."

"Anyone you know might be going parking?"

"I heard Jason and his girl talking about going to their spot at the lake. Not sure exactly where that spot is. Are they in trouble?"

"Let's hope not. Go home, son. Not only for your safety, but for that young lady with you." Jackson and Pressley would be heading to the lake.

Chapter Eighteen

Frank sat outside the movie theater. Who would he target tonight? The dark haired young man and the pretty redhead or the boy with the blonde? So many choices. Still, he needed to consider moving to a different city. Things were heating up in Texarkana, too much for his taste. The Feds would come back along with the reporters.

He tapped his finger on the steering wheel. Where was pretty Pressley from? That might be a good place to go. Somewhere no one knew him. She looked like a small town girl who would head home at the first sign of trouble.

Grinning, he started the engine and followed the redhead. While he drove, he contemplated a way of finding out Pressley's hometown. Excitement grew. Yep, law enforcement would be more scarce in a small town.

In one of the first newspapers, after Roy had been identified, there'd been a small write-up on the woman who had solved the case of The Phantom. Think, Frank!

The foolish young couple drove to the lake. Didn't they know there was a curfew? He shook his head at their rebellious idiocy. He parked on the side of the road, knowing which way the other car went by their taillights. Mask on and gun in hand, he set off through the woods for his last kill in Texarkana.

A laugh almost escaped him as two naked teenagers darted into the lake, squealing and splashing. Some people made it too easy.

Frank didn't try being quiet. He simply walked to the water's edge, aimed his gun, and pulled the trigger. As his first shot hit the young man, he remembered where Pressley was from. Grinning, he shot the girl.

~

"Jackson." Pressley gripped his arm. "That's the car Frank stole. He's here."

Backing up, Jackson slid out, leaving the engine running. He pulled a pocketknife from his pocket and stabbed the tires. "No sense making it easy for him to escape," he said, returning to the car. "Now to find—"

A shot rang out.

"Guess we know the general direction." Pressley wrapped her arms around herself as another shot sounded. Two more dead because they wouldn't follow a curfew.

"We stop here. If he doesn't know we're coming, we might catch him. Keep your gun ready." Jackson quietly opened his door, Pressley doing the same.

Staying only a step or two behind Jackson, she followed him along the edge of the road toward the shimmering lake. The form of a man turned, whistling like a white throated thrush silhouetted by the moonlight. He waved and made a dash for the trees.

"Stop!" Jackson gave chase.

Pressley turned toward the lake. The young people

floated naked face down in the water, their clothes in a pile on the shore.

"Come on."

"We can't leave them."

"They're dead. We'll come back."

Pressley sighed and followed Jackson. This was it. They'd catch Frank and put an end to his killing spree.

Jackson fired.

Frank bent over but kept running. They soon lost him in a thick stand of brush. Not giving up, Jackson pressed forward.

"He's bleeding." He pointed out wetness on a leaf. "Not fatally but hopefully enough to slow him down. I've not known many men his age who can move as fast as he can."

Amazing what someone could do when facing death. Pressley peered through the darkness expecting a bullet to strike her any second.

Pounding footsteps sounded to the right, causing Jackson to change direction. "He's headed for his car."

Good luck with that, Frank. Of course, the man was crazy enough to drive on the tire rims.

A bullet struck the tree near her head. A piece of bark struck her cheek. She brushed her hand against her face and pulled it away, blood on her fingers. Her hand shook at how close she'd come to dying, and she dropped to the ground.

Jackson hunkered down next to her. "I'm calling for backup. Maybe one of the other officers can intercept him. I can't put you in anymore danger."

"I'm fine." She struggled to her feet. "He'll get away."

"Most likely." He cupped her face in his hands, his

thumb brushing the scratch on her face. "It isn't worth you getting shot."

"It's worth it if it stops him."

"Not to me." He made the call for backup, then helped her to her feet and led her back to the lake.

Jackson waded into the water and pulled the girl out first before returning for the boy. Both had been shot in the chest. No one could have survived such a direct shot at close range.

Tears sprang to Pressley's eyes. When would it end? Frank was far worse than his relative had ever been. The insanity that drove the Becketts to such diabolical acts seemed to have festered like a cancer in Frank. Thankfully, as far as anyone knew, Frank was the last of his line.

Pressley covered the teens with their clothes and settled back to wait for the medical examiner.

~

Several hours passed before Jackson and Pressley could return to their vehicle. A piece of paper waved from under the windshield wiper. Jackson ripped it free and read, "I'll be seeing you."

"He's slashed your tires, too," Pressley said.

"Fair's fair, I guess." He handed her the note. "I'll call for a tow truck. Have a seat inside before you fall down."

Weariness etching her pretty face, she didn't argue and slid onto the passenger seat.

Another half an hour passed before the tow truck arrived, hooked up Jackson's car, then drove them home with promises to deliver the car in a few hours. Jackson nodded and put his hand on the small of Pressley's back, guiding her into the house.

"Let me tend to that scratch, then it's off to bed."

She sat in a kitchen chair. "It's already scabbing over."

"Still needs cleaning." He retrieved first aid items from the bathroom and rejoined her. "This might sting." He pressed a cotton ball soaked with antiseptic to her cheek.

She didn't make a sound, her gaze locked on his. "The note sounds as if he'll be making a move more specifically for us next."

"Yes." He was counting on it. If Frank came for them, they'd be ready. They weren't a couple of unsuspecting teenagers to be picked off like targets at the county fair. His gaze landed on Pressley's cheek. Maybe they were. It wouldn't happen again. He'd make sure it didn't. This woman had come to mean too much for him to lose her now. "There." He stood. "Time for bed. I've nothing pressing today, so sleep as long as you need to."

"Sleep sounds wonderful." She shuffled down the hall to her room.

After making sure the house was locked up tight, Jackson headed to his own room. Why hadn't Frank come for them at home as he had other couples? The man came and left like a ghost. With Jackson and Pressley sleeping, he could enter easy enough—something Jackson intended to remedy first thing. He'd meant to install an alarm system; now was the time.

With the reminder that Frank could break in so easily, Jackson grabbed his pillow and a blanket and moved to the sofa. Anyone trying to reach Pressley would have to go through him first.

The sun squeezing through the front window blinds woke him far too early. Jackson glanced at his watch and groaned. Only four hours of sleep. Not enough. He swung his legs off the sofa and padded to the kitchen, still fully dressed from last night. He'd crashed before even removing his shoes. After measuring coffee grounds into the pot, Jackson stared out the kitchen window, watching the city wake up around him.

A light thud outside signaled the delivery of the morning paper. He opened the door, glanced around, then grabbed the paper and returned to the kitchen table. The morning's headline reminded the residents about the mandatory curfew and the fine that resulted if it was violated. Hopefully, after hearing about last night's murders, people would actually listen.

Jackson understood not wanting to live in fear and being stuck in the house, but in order to stay alive, chances were better at home. He read how guns and ammo were flying off store shelves as residents armed themselves against a violent predator. Some were packing up and leaving town until the murders stopped. Good. Those were the ones who would be the safest.

He set the paper down, feeling like a failure as a police officer. Serve and protect. He hadn't done a lot of good in the protect department. At least Pressley was still okay.

Glancing up, he saw her standing in the doorway, her dark hair mussed around her face, and looking as gorgeous as he'd ever seen her despite the dark circles under her blue eyes.

"Morning." She made a beeline for the coffeepot. "The aroma woke me."

"I'm sorry." He grinned. Unlike himself, she'd changed into a large tee-shirt. While he suspected she wore shorts underneath, he couldn't tell since it fell to mid-thigh. "You're cute in the morning."

She shook her head. "I'm a mess."

"A beautiful mess."

She filled a cup of coffee and handed it to him, then poured another for herself and leaned against the counter. "What's on the agenda today? I noticed you slept on the sofa."

"An alarm system. I won't sleep until I have one installed."

"I'm surprised you haven't already."

"Intended to, but it wasn't a priority until now."

Carrying her coffee with her, she headed back down the hall, returning a few minutes later wearing jeans and a more fitting tee-shirt, her hair pulled into a ponytail. He preferred her hair down, if he were honest.

"I'm going to hit the shower."

"I'll fix breakfast." She refilled her coffee and opened the refrigerator.

When Jackson returned, a bacon and cheese omelet sat at his spot on the table. "My hero." He sat and dug in. "I had mushrooms?"

"Canned, but they do in a pinch." She smiled and sat across from him, tapping the newspaper. "Just like in the past with people buying guns and leaving."

He nodded. "Except this time, we know the identity of the man striking fear in everyone's hearts."

She reached across the table and put her hand over his. "We'll catch him. We were close last night. His luck can't last forever."

"Frank is smart enough to lead us on a chase for a good long while."

"Let's bring up using me as bait again."

"No." He pulled his hand from under hers. "Last

night was too close. You aren't a good enough shot to defend yourself if you face him alone."

"All I need is more practice. We can go to the range again after you order your alarm system." That stubborn look that said she wouldn't change her mind settled across her face. "People are dying. It's up to us to stop the killings."

She was right, but there had to be another way. "We can set a trap, but it will be with undercover officers."

"Yeah, that worked real well in 1946, didn't it?" She arched a brow. "Roy wasn't fooled in the least, and Frank is smarter than his relative ever was."

Jackson's shoulders slumped. They might have to do the very thing he hated doing, and that would put Pressley directly into the path of a killer.

Chapter Nineteen

Frank entered Applewood a little after ten the next evening. Using Google Maps, he'd found a hunting cabin that would serve as his temporary home. Since it wasn't hunting season, he ought to be able to stay there undiscovered.

But first, he needed to light a fire in Pressley's hometown.

A thrill shot through him as he entered new territory. This town wasn't under a curfew, and while it had only around three thousand residents, he'd have plenty of opportunities.

There wouldn't be as many young couples out on a weeknight, but it was summer. He drove slowly looking for a place people would gather, smiling as he passed a ball field. Two teams of girls played softballs, and there were a lot of young men cheering from the sidelines.

Frank parked and exited his car, pulling his cap low. No need for his mask yet. No one in this town knew him, so he could scout freely. He approached a young man cheering on the pitcher. "She's good."

The young man grinned. "That's my girl. She's the best."

"Looks like they're winning. Plan on celebrating afterward?"

He turned to Frank. "That's a strange question."

"Is it?" Frank shrugged. "I'm new to town. Not sure where someone would go to celebrate or even to get a good meal."

"Maria's is good. They serve all kinds of food." He turned back to the game. "You can find it on Main Street, but they're closed now. The game is in overtime, or we'd be out of here by now."

Frank nodded and returned to his car. He drummed his fingers on the steering wheel. Should he wait for this young man or find someone else? What if he simply dropped his girlfriend off at her house? Frank would have wasted valuable time. Was it a chance he wanted to take?

In order to lure Pressley back home, he needed to make the morning's paper.

A young couple peeled away from the crowd and strolled hand in hand away from the field, cutting across a large green area. A road stretched across the other side.

Frank smiled and drove away. He'd make a brazen move that night, catching the couple as they stepped onto the far sidewalk. He parked and shot them the moment they stepped off the grass onto the cement, then sped away. Not his usual way of doing things, but Pressley would know he was the one who'd taken the shots.

~

Pressley woke to the sight of Jackson standing in the doorway of her room. A newspaper dangled from his hand. "What is it?" She shoved her hair out of her eyes.

"A shooting in your hometown."

"Applewood?" She bolted upright.

"It isn't the same MO. These two were shot leaving a ball game. They're expected to survive." He handed her the paper.

After scanning the article, she climbed out of bed. "We have to go. This was Frank. He wants us to follow him." She grabbed her suitcase from under the bed and started tossing in her clothes. "There's an annual feed-the-homeless event in a few days. Frank is bound to show up there. We can volunteer to help and blend in that way. What?" She paused at the stoic look on Jackson's face.

"I don't like this at all."

She sighed and stood in front of him, taking his hands in hers. "It's all coming to an end. Can't you feel it? It's almost over."

"You might die."

"My life will be worth losing if it stops Frank from killing." She reached up and cupped his face. "We have to do this, Jackson."

"I know." He stepped away and went back down the hall.

Her heart warmed to know he cared, but she couldn't let his worry interfere with them stopping a crazed killer. Did she want to die? No, but putting herself out there was the only way.

Pressley finished packing and headed to the kitchen for coffee and a quick breakfast. She wanted to be on the road as soon as possible. In the living room, Jackson was telling someone he'd be gone for a while. The chief, most likely. Hopefully, the chief would alert the small department in Applewood. The peaceful town wasn't equipped to handle a rash of murders.

A few minutes later, Jackson joined her in the

kitchen. "I'm free to go. Let me pack a few things, and I'll be ready to leave."

"Looks like you'll be staying with me now." She smiled around the rim of her cup.

The corner of his mouth twitched. "Only fair that it's my turn to use up all the hot water in the shower."

"I do not!"

He winked and headed down the hall.

She sobered, knowing their banter was only to ease the anxiety over the reason they were packing. Now that things were winding down, what would she do once Frank was behind bars? Stay in Applewood or follow Jackson back to Texarkana? Pressley knew what she wanted to do, but he still hadn't asked her to stay.

Hinting wasn't enough. She needed to hear the question. Pressley set her cup down and scrambled some eggs, added cheese, and rolled them into tortillas. Breakfast burritos could be eaten in the car easy enough. She wrapped them in foil to keep them warm as Jackson joined her again, this time with a duffel bag in one hand.

"I'm ready."

She poured coffee into two thermoses. "Let's go."

He led the way, then locked his house behind her. "I never had time to order the alarm system."

"We don't need it here any longer, and my grandmother's house has one. She remained paranoid after 1946."

~

Jackson munched on his breakfast as they drove north. If they didn't succeed in catching Frank, would he move on in a few days, staying just ahead of capture? Would he ever stop on his own? Most likely not. Most serial killers didn't.

Cutting a sideways glance at the woman beside him, Jackson would do everything in his power to keep her safe…even if it meant taking the bullet meant for her. "Do you want to go home first or stop at the station?" he asked.

"Whichever you think best."

"We'll want to question the survivors and those attending the ball game. Someone saw Frank."

She nodded. "We've a full day ahead of us."

Too full. Hopefully, the chief of police in Applewood would be glad for their help and not feel as if they were stepping on his toes. "We'll go to the station first, introduce ourselves, and make sure there isn't something they want us to do."

"You think they'll ask us to stay out of it?"

"Maybe."

"I won't." She hiked her chin, a glint of determination in her eyes. "I'm valuable to this investigation."

"I see that, and you see it. Let's hope they do too."

The sun was high in the sky when they pulled in front of a metal building housing the small police department. "Let me do the talking," Jackson said. "One officer to another."

"Okay." She followed him into the air-conditioned building.

An officer sat behind a desk instead of a receptionist. "May I help you?"

"I'm Detective Hudson out of Texarkana." Jackson showed his badge.

"Your chief called. Seems you might know something about our shooting last night."

"A bit. Is your chief in?"

"Chief Stone is in there. Go on." He jerked his head toward a door on his left. "He's expecting you."

This might be easy after all. Jackson rapped knuckles on the door, then entered when told to, introducing himself and Pressley.

The chief, a middle-aged man in good shape, smiled and nodded at Pressley. "Good to see you again, Pressley. Have a seat, both of you. Tell me what you know. Chief Rawlings told me the two of you are getting close to stopping this guy. If we do have The Phantom on our hands, we're grateful for any help."

Some of the tension left Jackson's shoulders as he and Pressley took their seats. He explained what they knew about Frank. "We'd like to speak to the victims and those attending the softball game."

"Here's the list. We've already questioned them, but you might learn something new. This young man—" he pointed to a Seth Moore, "said he might have spoken to your man. Said he asked some strange questions. No one else noticed Beckett."

"Then we'll focus our efforts on Mr. Moore." Jackson handed the sheet to Pressley. "Do we have free rein, sir?"

"Do what you need to in order to stop this man. I know Miss Taylor, her grandmother, too. This is a small town. A newcomer will stick out."

Jackson stood and shook the chief's hand. "Thank you." He was counting on the grapevine to help them.

"It's good to see you again." Pressley held out her hand.

"Looks like you've shaken up a hornet's nest, little lady. Rumor has it that your grandmother did the same back in the day. You be careful." The chief returned her handshake.

"I intend to." Pressley led the way from the office. "You can stay in my grandmother's room. I never found the time to move my things in there. You'll have your own bathroom."

"I'll sleep wherever." Jackson had been glad to hear about an alarm system. No more sofa sleeping for a while.

His room was more than adequate with a queen-sized bed. He set his bag on the crocheted bedspread and rubbed his hands briskly down his face. Jackson doubted they'd learn much from the victims, but they had to speak with them anyway. He went in search of Pressley, finding her in a room that matched his only without an en suite bathroom. "Ready?"

"Yes. Here's the alarm code." She handed him a slip of paper.

"One, two, three, four? Really?"

"I've been meaning to change it."

"I suggest we do so before we leave." He raised his brows. "A five-year-old could figure this out."

"Grandma wanted to keep things simple." She scribbled another set of numbers on the paper. "Ten, nine, eight, seven. Better?"

"Not by much."

"Are you hungry? We could stop at Marie's, eat a burger or something before questioning Seth Moore."

"Sounds good to me." His stomach growled.

The restaurant had painted murals on the wall and mismatched tables and chairs. Quaint. He hoped the food was good.

An older woman led them to a table and handed them menus. "I'm Sue. Good to see you again, Pressley.

You've been gone a while. Can I help you?"

"I'll take a diet soda," Pressley said, glancing at the menu.

"Regular." Jackson pulled a photo of Frank from his pocket. "Have you seen this man?"

Sue studied the picture. "He came in for breakfast this morning, except he wasn't wearing a suit and his hair was shaggy. I've never seen him before, and I know everyone around these parts."

"Anywhere a newcomer could stay and not be easily found?"

"Sweetie, these hills are full of hunting cabins. If I wanted to hide, I'd pick one of them this time of year. It'd be a miracle to find him."

That's what Jackson was afraid of.

"You here to help with the feeding?" Sue asked.

"Never miss it." Pressley smiled. "I'll have the bacon mushroom burger. If you see this man again, will you call me?"

"What's he done?"

"He's a serial killer," Jackson answered. "The one who killed in Texarkana the last few weeks."

The woman went as pale as the pad of paper in her hand. "What have you gotten yourself into, Pressley? Why bring trouble to our town?"

Chapter Twenty

Pressley's throat clogged. Sue was right. Pressley had brought trouble to her small town. "We'll put him away." She prayed they would.

"I sure hope so. We don't need this. There are people who were children in 1946. They remember the horror of that time." She scowled and dropped some napkins on the table before leaving to place their orders.

"This isn't your fault." Jackson entwined her fingers with his. "Frank would've snapped if you hadn't pursued The Phantom case."

"You don't know that. My interfering was the trigger."

"Insanity has no reason."

She appreciated his attempt to cheer her up. Unfortunately, it didn't work.

The rest of lunch was silent except for Jackson praising his double cheeseburger. When they'd finished, paid, and left a healthy tip, they headed to the address given for Seth Moore.

The only consolation Pressley had that morning was that they were actively hunting Frank, and his last two victims had survived his attack. She'd hold onto that fact for as long as possible.

Seth lived with his parents in a small white boarded house. He opened the door before Jackson could knock. "Can I help you?"

"I'm Detective Hudson from Texarkana PD, and this is Pressley Taylor. We'd like to ask you a few questions about the man you spoke with last night."

He stepped onto the front porch, pulling the door closed behind him. "Mind if we talk out here? My mother is sleeping. Last night's shooting gave her stress." He motioned for them to sit in two metal chairs while he perched on the porch railing.

Pressley could imagine. A mother's heart would shudder at how close her son had been to a killer. She sat in one of the chairs, Jackson in the other.

"Can you tell us what you spoke with him about?" Jackson asked.

"The dude was weird. Asked about good places to hang out or go eat. Everyone knows that nothing's open that late. Then, he went and sat in his car for a few minutes until Buddy and his girl left the game."

"He followed them?"

Seth shook his head. "No, he drove off."

"Did you see who shot your friends?"

"No. Just heard the shots. The game stopped. There was screaming. People ducked to the ground or hid behind things. This doesn't happen here. It's left everyone a bit whacked out, you know?"

Pressley knew how they all felt. If she hadn't engrained herself into the case and been exposed to violence, she'd have done the same and hid.

"Did this man mention where he might be staying?"

"Not a word."

Jackson rose to his feet. "You're a lucky young man. Please don't go out after dark with your girl until this man is caught."

"Don't worry. My parents won't let me go to my room alone after last night. I hope you catch this guy fast. Football practice starts soon."

"We'll do our best." Jackson led Pressley back to the car. "I guess the hospital is next."

"Seth wasn't a lot of help, was he?"

"Hopefully the other two will be." Jackson followed her directions to the hospital in a neighboring town and parked in the mostly empty parking lot. "Not a lot of sick people here, is there?"

"Not at this hospital. In the other one, you'd wait hours to be seen in the ER." She shoved her door open and climbed out. Memories of her grandmother's last days assailed her the moment the double doors slid open. It hadn't always been easy being the caregiver, but she wouldn't trade a minute of the time she'd had with her.

"It's good to see you again, Pressley." Sharon, a classmate from high school, sat behind the receptionist desk. "You feeling okay?"

"I'm fine. We aren't here for me."

Jackson showed his badge. "We're here to see Buddy Mayfield and Melissa Byrnes."

"Which one would you like to see first?" She scribbled their room numbers on a post-it note. "I'll have to call and make sure the doctor isn't with them."

"It doesn't matter." Jackson smiled.

Sharon blushed. Pressley smiled, knowing the handsome man had that effect on most of the women he flashed that gorgeous grin at. Sharon confirmed it was all right to see both of them and pointed in the direction they should go.

"This place is a maze," Jackson said as they turned their third corner.

"If I hadn't spent so much time here last year, I'd be lost, too." Pressley led him to the patient wing. The first room was Buddy's.

He sat up in bed, his left shoulder wrapped, and idly flipped channels on the television. Buddy glanced up, then frowned. "Thought maybe they were finally bringing my lunch."

"Sorry." Jackson introduced them. "Feel up to some questions?"

"Sure. I'm bored out of my mind."

"Tell us about last night."

"Melissa and I got tired of the game. It went into overtime and she had to be home, it being a school night and all. We cut across the field to save time. A truck pulled up to the curb, a man shot us, then drove away whistling."

Pressley glanced at Jackson. "A bird call?"

"Yeah. Real creepy."

"Can you describe the man?" Jackson asked.

"He wore a hoodie. I wasn't paying much attention to him. If I brought Melissa home late again, her parents would ground her, and it was already ten. That's when she was supposed to be home." Tears welled in his eyes. "If we'd left the game earlier, this wouldn't have happened."

"Son, there's no predicting what this madman will do. You couldn't have known. Just thank God you're still alive."

"Is this the same man who killed all those people down in Texarkana?"

"Yes."

"Why is he here?" Buddy's brow lowered.

"To get me," Pressley murmured.

~

Melissa told them less than Buddy had. She'd been so worried about getting home she didn't know anything other than she'd been shot and fell to the ground. "I'm sorry." Her lip quivered.

Pressley patted her hand. "It's okay. You concentrate on getting better."

Outside, Jackson wanted to punch something. They were so close to Frank, yet farther than they've ever been. The forest around Applewood was too thick for a pilot in a helicopter to see through. They wouldn't get that lucky again.

"What does a white-throated thrush sound like?" Pressley opened her car door and peered over the top.

"I can't imitate it, but I can look it up on my phone." Jackson searched until he found the sound, then played it. "It is creepy."

"At least now I'll know to run if I hear it." She laughed. "Even if it's a real bird, I won't be taking any chances."

"That's my girl." He enjoyed the flush that spread across her cheeks. "Ready to head home, order a pizza, and chill for the rest of the night?" They couldn't do anything more until Frank reared his ugly head.

"That sounds wonderful, after a stop at the church to sign up for the feeding-the-homeless event."

"Which one? I counted at least five."

"I'll show you." She smiled. "I'm glad I won't miss out this year."

Jackson was, too, but for different reasons. His gut

told him Frank would be there somewhere, watching. Pressley would encounter people who'd be excited to see her back home and willing to help out. "Folks sure know everyone here, don't they?"

"If your family has been here long enough, yes," she said. "It's both a blessing and a curse. I couldn't do anything wrong without someone tattling on me to my parents."

"You did something wrong?" He tilted his head, smiling.

"I wasn't always the good girl you see before you." She grinned back. "Now, how about that peaceful evening you promised me?"

Something Jackson was more than happy to give. He supposed Pressley must have had a bit of a wild side not to run screaming into the night with the recent murders, not to mention the fact Frank wanted her.

The next morning, he woke feeling a bit disoriented until he realized where he was. The aroma of coffee and frying bacon drifted to his room. He quite liked playing house with Pressley, and it didn't matter which house. What man wouldn't want to wake up to a beautiful woman who wanted to make the world a better place?

Jackson flung off the thin sheet he'd covered himself with and padded to the kitchen. When Pressley turned with wide eyes, he rushed back to the bedroom to put on a shirt. He'd grown comfortable enough with her to forget proper behavior, it seemed. He chuckled at the look of shock on her face, and his grin widened imagining he might have seen a flicker of appreciation in her blue eyes.

A few minutes later, he tried again and received a smile and a cup of coffee. "You're going to spoil me."

"Like you spoiled me when it was your house. Sit. Breakfast will be finished soon."

"You seem pleased."

"Newspaper didn't report anymore shootings or deaths."

So, the other night's shooting was merely a ploy to bring Pressley home. Jackson had known that, but he sure didn't like the idea. Frank would lie in wait, then grab her, and Jackson might not be able to stop him. The thought scared him enough to make the coffee bitter in his mouth.

"What's wrong?" Pressley glanced over from the stove.

"Just thinking."

"Not good thoughts if your expression is any indication." She set a cheese and bacon omelet in front of him. "We'll find him, Jackson. Soon. I know we will."

He exhaled heavily and started eating. Jackson wanted to believe they'd apprehend Frank without him harming Pressley, but signs were strongly against that happening.

"I don't want anything to happen to you." He forced the words through a tortured throat.

"I'm of the same sentiment. You're in as much danger as I am. If Frank were to take you out first, I'd be easier to reach." She sat across from him with a plate of her own. "Any plans for today?"

He forced a smile at her attempt to change the subject. "Guess we drive around and try to find his latest hiding place."

"Good. That also lets us be seen, although I still believe the feeding event tomorrow is our best bet for contact." She cut into her breakfast.

"I'm going to ask that some plainclothes police officers be there. If Frank does show up, we'll need backup."

"It might scare him off."

"That's a chance we have to take. I'm assuming there'll be young people there, right? Victims for him to target?"

She nodded. "Several church youth groups will be serving."

If Frank couldn't get to Pressley, he'd find someone else. "Any chance of calling off tomorrow's event?"

"No. It's an annual thing. People around these parts won't run scared. You can bet there will be a few, even a pastor or two, packing."

Great. Last thing they needed was a shootout with civilians. Jackson shook his head and finished eating. When he was done, he headed to take a shower and make a plan on how to spot Frank before he spotted them.

Chapter Twenty-one

Jackson stayed close by Pressley's side as she carried a stack of paper plates to a table in the shade of a large oak tree. Serving wouldn't start for another hour, and already a line formed. He doubted all those were homeless, but times were hard, and no one would be turned away that wanted a meal.

Where are you, Frank? He studied a man in a hoodie leaning against the side of the church. Too thin, but the day was also way too hot to be wearing a hoodie. If Frank wore one, he'd stick out like a sore thumb unless he found one as raggedy as these people wore. Jackson didn't think the man would think that far ahead. The people of Applewood wouldn't recognize him unless they'd closely followed the news out of Texarkana. He'd come without a disguise.

"Could you fetch the tray of hot dogs?" Pressley glanced up. "I promise to stay right here unless Pastor Dave wants me for something else."

Hating to leave her, Jackson rushed into the fellowship building, grabbed the tray, and carried it outside. His breathing returned to normal to see Pressley where he'd left her talking to another woman. He'd just set down the tray when a supervisor sent him back for potato salad sitting in a bin of ice. So, he'd been cast as gopher. At least it helped him know who were the workers and who weren't.

A scream at the end of the parking lot froze him in his tracks. He shook his head to see a young man teasing a teenage girl. Why did girls have to shriek?

"Thank you." Pressley smiled up at him as he set down the potato salad. "This is my friend, Marley. We've known each other since grade school."

Jackson nodded at the cute blonde. "Nice to meet you."

"Pressley told me y'all are trying to catch a killer." Marley cocked her head. "Sounds deliciously dangerous."

Strange thing to say. He frowned. "Not sure I agree with you on the delicious part."

"Pressley's grandma talked about The Phantom all the time. Made it hard for Pressley to socialize much." Marley winked. "She had to sneak."

"Stop telling all my secrets." Pressley laughed. "I've already told him I wasn't always a good girl. He doesn't need to know exactly how bad I was."

"Oh, the stories I could tell." Marley sidestepped to avoid Pressley's playful punch aimed at her arm.

Jackson enjoyed seeing Pressley carefree, the worry lines erased from her face. She deserved time to enjoy herself. While she caught up with her friend, he strolled down the line of waiting people, studying them while still keeping an eye on the two women behind the serving table. He noticed handguns in holsters on belts of several of the church members and even more rifles in gunracks hanging on the back window of trucks. There were enough firearms to start a war.

"These people like their guns." Chief Stone stepped next to him, wearing jeans and a button-up shirt. "Besides myself, there are three other officers here out of uniform. Borrowed them from neighboring cities. You really think the man will show?"

"I do." Jackson motioned his head toward Pressley. "He'll come for her."

"I'll make sure we have eyes on her the whole time."

"I appreciate that, Chief."

"Watch your back." He strolled away heading toward a row of porta potties set up on the edge of a large grassy area.

Jackson moved to the corner of the church and stood in the shadow of the building, hoping it provided some protection from being spotted. The place gave him a good vantage point of not only the table where Pressley stood, but the line of people and those milling around the area.

Occasionally, he'd stiffened, catching sight of a man with the same build as Frank, but relaxed when that person would turn and Jackson could see his face. Were they wrong about Frank showing up there? Was he lying in wait somewhere else? Somewhere less crowded?

If Jackson was the predator, he'd hide in plain sight. This gathering of people was the perfect opportunity. With the roughhousing of teen boys and the giggles and shrieks of the girls they tried to impress, a scream would be lost. No one would give the sound a second thought.

He glanced back to Pressley and the future once Frank was caught. Would she want to stay in Applewood or would she return to Texarkana with him if he asked? Could he stay there, leaving behind his job? Jackson didn't have family to hold him in the southern part of the state. Yeah, he could stay here. He might actually enjoy small town life, especially with Pressley at his side.

The line started moving. Pressley smiled and spoke with each person she handed a plate to. Jackson's growing admiration and love for her grew even more. He'd never met a kinder woman and laughed, thinking of her as a rebellious teen. She'd always be sweet, stubborn, determined Pressley to him.

He tried to pick out the plain-clothed law enforcement and was relieved that he couldn't. They blended in well with the others. Frank shouldn't be in the least suspicious. So where was he?

~

Frank continued watching from the hole he'd poked in the wall of one of the porta potties as Pressley served plate after plate of food. His stomach growled despite the stench of his hiding place.

A few times, someone had tried the door where he hid but moved on when they found it locked. It had been hours and Frank still hadn't found the opportunity to slip out. Sweat dripped down his face and back. All he needed was for Hudson to look away. Just for a second, so Frank could sneak out and hide behind the church near the dumpsters.

There. Someone called for Hudson's help with a couple of men arguing near the end of the food line. Frank darted from his hiding place and rounded the church. Breathing a sigh of relief at a breeze drying the sweat from his face, he leaned against the red brick and waited.

~

"Could you take that bag to the dumpster?" Marley

asked. "It's overflowing, and we still have a lot of people to feed. If I trip over it one more time, I'll scream. I can handle this for a few minutes."

Pressley glanced around to ask Jackson to help, but he was holding apart two men yelling at each other. She shook her head and tied the black bag closed, then slung it over her shoulder and trudged toward the dumpsters.

Hefting the bag over the edge, she turned. The eerie song of a white-throated thrush froze her in her tracks.

Frank stepped from behind the dumpster and pointed a gun at her head. "Time to go. Scream, and I'll shoot you where you stand, then hunt down Hudson. I'll make sure to kill him real slow."

"Go where?" She forced the question from a dry throat.

"I've a car waiting. Cut through those trees. I'm right behind you."

Pressley took a deep breath, sent up a prayer, and headed into the woods and across a pasture high with grass to where a white sedan was parked. She slipped her hand into her pocket and made sure her cell phone was on. Jackson would be able to track her as long as she had service. Unfortunately, she'd left her grandmother's pistol in Jackson's car. She knew Frank would show up but thought there would be enough people around to keep her safe. Stupid move.

"Driver's seat," Frank said. "Can't have you trying anything." He reached around her to open the door. The man stunk.

Pressley held her breath until he stepped back, then got in.

Frank kept the gun trained on her through the windshield as he moved to the passenger seat. Once inside, he gave her directions to an old vacant motel. So he'd been staying two miles from Pressley's house waiting for his chance. Good. She'd have cell service.

"Why not kill me now?" She cut him a sideways glance.

"I have plans for some fun before I do. The same kind of fun I've had with some of the girls I've killed. We'll have more time than I had with them." He gave a lecherous grin. "Imagine how crazy Hudson will be when he discovers your body."

Pressley shuddered. *Do whatever it takes to survive* was what her grandmother would tell her. She intended to do just that. Pressley was no violet. She could endure whatever she needed to until Jackson came for her. *Please, God, help me endure.*

Frank ordered her to park the car behind the dilapidated building, then ushered her toward the furthest room. The shattered door handle told of how he'd gained entry.

The room held no furniture, just a stained orange shag carpet, a couple of plastic bags full of food, and a dented milk crate. She didn't want to know what had caused the stains.

"Sit down." Frank waved the gun to a corner of the room. "I sure wish you could have grabbed a plate of that food. All I have here are chips and gas station sausage." He sat on the crate and pulled a sausage stick from a nearby grocery bag. "I'd offer you one, but I saw you eat a hot dog."

Keep talking, crazy man. As long as he talked, he wasn't hurting her. She wrapped her arms around her bent knees and fought to keep fear at bay. Hurry, Jackson. She glanced around for something to use as a weapon. Nothing except the crate Frank sat on. It might work if she could reach it without him shooting her.

"You're awfully quiet for a nosy woman."

She shrugged. "You aren't exactly the type of person I care to have a conversation with."

"Aren't you curious about why I've been killing like Roy did?" He grinned.

Fine. She'd humor him. "Okay, why?"

"It started as nothing more than you ruining my good family name. Turns out, I enjoy the killing, messing around with the girls before I shoot them. It's a strange sense of power to see the fear in their eyes."

"Roy was shell-shocked. You're simply insane."

"I'd say it runs in the family, wouldn't you?" His grin widened as he popped the last of the sausage in his mouth and grabbed a bag of chips from the bag. "You be nice, and I'll make your death quick. You're real smart for such a pretty thing. Too bad you messed with the wrong people."

"Yeah, too bad." Pressley rested her chin on her knees and kept her gaze locked on him in case he made a move toward her. She felt strangely calm for someone about to die.

Frank must have thought so, too, because he narrowed his eyes. "Why aren't you hysterical?"

"I'm not that type."

"Most women would be crying and pleading for their life."

She shrugged. "You're bigger than I am, have a gun, and have no qualms about killing. What good would it do for me to beg?"

"See? I said you were smart. Maybe I'll keep you around for a while."

That thought scared her more than the thought of him killing her.

Chapter Twenty-two

"Where's Pressley?" Jackson approached Marley at a run. "She was supposed to stay with you."

The woman glanced around. "She took out the garbage a while ago. I thought she was with you when she didn't return."

Jackson's heart stopped a mere second before he dashed around the corner of the church. No sign of her. Why would she have gone off alone?

He whirled as footsteps pounded behind him. The chief and one of the other officers stopped next to him. "Marley told us Miss Taylor is gone." Chief Stone ordered the other cop to search the church.

"I shouldn't have left her to stop that fight." Jackson ran his hands through his hair, not caring if he looked like a porcupine. He'd failed to keep Pressley safe. "If her cell phone is on, we can track her. Get someone on that."

Chief Stone called for another officer to take over that task. "Don't worry, Hudson. We'll find her. If he wanted her dead right away, we'd be standing over her body."

Small consolation, but the man was right. Pressley

was more than likely still alive, hopefully unharmed. *Wait for me, sweetheart. I'm coming.*

He returned to where a tearful Marley cleared off the serving table. "I'm sorry," she said, sobbing. "It's my fault. I asked her to take out the garbage."

"It isn't your fault." Jackson put a consoling hand on her shoulder. "He would have found her another way."

"But I made it easy." She buried her face in his chest. Although he patted her back, it was Pressley his arms wanted to hold.

Once the woman calmed down and returned to work, Jackson went in search of the chief. "Anything?"

"We've pinged her phone at an abandoned motel. Let's go." They raced for the waiting vehicles.

The signal ended before they pulled into the driveway. No cars sat in the parking lot. A quick search of the rear of the building yielded fresh tire tracks. They were gone.

Jackson sagged against the wall, knowing Pressley's time was limited. Wherever she was now, she had no cell service. She was on her own.

Trying not to panic, he studied the ground to determine which direction they'd gone. Impossible once Frank was on the highway. Usually, Jackson kept a clear head in intense situations, but Pressley had turned his world around. He almost lost all reason, thinking he'd lost her before he had a chance to tell her how he felt. Jackson prayed in those minutes more than he'd prayed in years. "Where could they have gone?"

"You know this man better than we do, Hudson," the chief said. "Think."

"Where do the teens hang out? Is there a special

place they like to go parking?"

"There's a spot up the mountain and tons of country roads with ponds and lakes. Without a signal from her phone, we'll be going around like headless chickens."

"Get a chopper in the air. It's something. It's the middle of the day, so visibility shouldn't be too bad if they're around water." If they were in the woods, only a ton of luck would lead to spotting them. Hope started to trickle through his fingers like water. "I'm going to start at the nearest possible place and keep widening the circle. How fast can we organize a group of volunteers to help us search?"

"An hour minimum. We've a phone chain that will spread the word fast enough. We'll have everyone meet back at the church."

Jackson nodded. "Let's get started and pray Pressley has that long."

A little less than an hour they had twenty volunteers, all armed, all dressed in camouflage as if they were going deer hunting. He shrugged. They *were* hunting. The only difference was the one they sought walked on two legs.

The chief spread a map over the hood of a squad car and sent people to every spot he could think of where teens went parking. Jackson and the chief would start with a small lake named Evergreen because of the algae. *Please, God, shower them with some luck.*

Each team was handed walkie-talkies. "Give a shout out if you see Beckett or Miss Taylor, and help will come running," the chief said. "Under no circumstance are you to engage with the suspect. Do not shoot unless your life is in danger. If this man is not with Miss Taylor, and you kill him, we might never find her."

Her body he meant, sending ice through Jackson's

veins. The more time that passed, the less likely they'd find Pressley alive.

~

Frank stared at the woman in the corner. Beautiful and brave. Now that he had her, killing her seemed pointless. His life had become worthless other than his thirst for murder. With Pressley dead, he still couldn't return to the life he'd once had.

He pushed to his feet and paced the small room, her eyes warily watching his every move. But then again, getting rid of her, much like Roy wanted to do with his former fiancée after the woman had broken up with him, would be a period at the end of a very long sentence that started in 1946. Both women had upended the Beckett men's lives to the point nothing could return to normal. Shooting her outright was boring. "Get up. We're going to the lake we passed on the way here."

"Why?" Her eyes narrowed.

"To play a game of chase." Excitement reared its big, beautiful head. He'd be at a disadvantage since she knew the area, but oh, what fun the reward of killing her would be.

~

Frank nudged Pressley toward the water's edge. "Strip down to your underwear."

She glared. At least he wasn't having her completely disrobe and the spring temperatures wouldn't have her succumbing to the elements. Other than mild embarrassment, she'd be fine. Grateful she wore modest underwear, she disrobed and tossed one of her shoes into the water, wishing she could somehow keep her phone with her. Hopefully, the shoe was enough for Jackson to know she was around.

Cursing, Frank gathered up her other clothing items and put them in the trunk of the car. "With you barefoot and not fully clothed, we'll be more equal."

"Then I should have a gun."

"Not a chance. I'll give you to the count of ten. When I find you, I'll shoot you. Then we're finished."

At least he'd changed his mind about rape. She'd take whatever small favor he offered. She knew the area due to many evening parties as a teen. Before he said one, she was sprinting through the trees, mentally counting to ten, knowing her white bra and panties would shine like a beacon. She needed a hiding place and a weapon.

Spotting a fallen tree limb the size of her wrist, she bent and retrieved it before plunging through thick underbrush. The landscape had changed a bit but not enough for her to feel lost. She knew where the highway was and headed in that direction, hoping to flag down a passing car.

Ten. He'd be coming. She'd hoped to have put more distance between them. Without slowing her pace, she veered right toward a thick stand of trees and plastered her back against the trunk of the largest one. Clutching the tree limb like a club, she waited, her heart pounding so hard she feared he'd hear her. *Lord, give me strength.*

She tensed and held her breath every time a twig snapped or a leaf rustled. Each time a squirrel or rabbit crossed her path, her breath hitched. Come on, Frank. She'd left a trail a blind man could follow.

A chopper circled overhead. She fought the urge to run into the open and wave her arms.

A white-throated thrush whistled nearby, or was it Frank? Her heart hammered in her throat. The snap of another twig, louder this time. Pressley raised the tree limb over her head. She refused to die in these woods at the hands of Frank Beckett.

He stepped into view and she brought the limb down on his head with all the strength she could muster. He crumbled to the ground, dropping the gun, and grabbed her ankle, pulling her down with him.

She screamed and kicked, aiming for his head.

Cursing, he fought to get on top of her, switching his hand from her ankle to her neck.

Spots swam in front of her eyes. She screamed and raised the limb again, bringing it down as hard as she could, striking him in the side of the head. She shoved him off her and scrambled to her feet, her gaze searching frantically for the weapon.

Pressley dropped the limb and plucked the gun from a pile of decaying pine needles. "Get up." She aimed the weapon at his head.

"You won't shoot me." He glared up at her.

"Don't try me. I didn't take shooting lessons for nothing. Now, get up. Don't make me say it again." Her hands shook.

He struggled to his hands and knees, then pushed to his feet. "Go ahead and shoot."

"I'd rather you spend the rest of your life in prison. Back to the car." She jammed the barrel into his back.

Frank marched back to the lake, keeping his hands over his head. Once there, he asked, "Now what?"

"Get my clothes."

He unlocked the trunk and handed her the clothes.

"Get in."

"What?" His brow lowered.

"You heard me."

Cursing, he climbed into the trunk, not an easy feat

for a man his size. Pressley grinned down at him before slamming the trunk closed. She dressed and retrieved her soaked shoe before returning to the car and pounding on the trunk. "Thanks for the fun."

Another curse was the response.

Pressley climbed on top of the trunk and held her phone up, trying to get a signal. One bar. It was enough. She dialed Jackson, pressed the speaker button, and held the phone up.

"Pressley?"

"It's me. I'm all right."

"Where's Frank?"

"I locked him in the trunk. Tell the chief I'm at Evergreen."

"I'm almost there."

When his car came into sight, she set the gun down and raced toward him, throwing herself at him when he exited the car and wrapped her arms and legs around him. "How did you know where I was?"

"My heart led me here. I said I'd start at the closest spot." He squeezed her tight. "I didn't expect it to be this easy."

"Speak for yourself." She cupped his face and kissed him. "I am so glad to see you," she whispered against his lips.

Jackson slid her down the length of him, never losing contact with her lips. He raised his head. "No more so than I am."

Chief Stone cleared his throat. "Mind giving me the key to the trunk so I can take Beckett into custody?"

Pressley laughed and dug the keys from her pocket, tossing them to him. He caught them in one hand and headed for the car.

"It's over," she said.

"Yes." Jackson grinned. "You gave me quite a scare."

"The sound of a white-throated thrush will send shivers down my spine every time I hear the sound."

"At least you're alive to hear it."

"There is that." She peered into his eyes wanting very much to tell him how she felt. Now was not the time or the place. It could wait until they were home.

The chief hauled Frank from the trunk and cuffed him before putting him in the backseat of the squad car. "That white car was reported stolen a couple of days ago. Why don't you two drive it to the church? I'll have the owner retrieve it there."

"Sounds good." Jackson wrapped his arm around Pressley's waist. "Let's take this back, pick up my car, then take you home."

"I'm ready."

On the drive to church, she told him how Frank had captured her, took her to the motel, then gave her to the count of ten to chase her through the woods. "I clubbed him with a tree branch, then took his gun."

"That's my girl." Jackson reached over and squeezed her hand. "You're amazing, Pressley Taylor."

"I come from good stock." His words dispelled the last of the day's tension. She was safe, and Frank would go to prison for the rest of his life if he didn't receive the death penalty. Either way, he would not kill innocent people again.

At home, Jackson sat her on the sofa and took both her hands in his. "We need to talk."

"About?" This was it. He was going to tell her he was leaving. She stiffened, then steeled herself for heartbreak.

"I love you, Pressley. I don't care if you want to stay here or go to Texarkana. As long as I'm with you, the where doesn't matter."

She glanced around the living room of her grandmother's house. "I love Applewood, but I love you more. Wherever you want to go, I want to go."

His gaze searched her face. "Then we stay. If I can't get a job with the police department here, I'll find a different one. I'd like to give small town life a chance if you'll be my wife. Say you'll marry me."

"I'll marry you." She smiled. "I'd be a fool to let you go."

"And a fool is one thing you're not." He gave a crooked grin. "I don't have a ring. We can pick one out together."

"Why don't you stop talking and kiss me before I change my mind?"

He laughed and pulled her into his lap. "I'll be kissing you until my last breath." His lips claimed hers.

The End

Dear Reader,

In 1946, as soldiers returned home from the Second World War, a killer terrorized the southern town of Texarkana but was never apprehended. Some say he was a petty car thief who died in prison a year later. Others say the killer was a young man just out of college.

This is my version of what *might* have happened had The Phantom not disappeared. My version of my theory, then continuing the story into the present. While the killings are based on actual historical facts, much has been fabricated in my story. There was no Pressley Taylor or Mary Ann Warren who tried to find the answers. We don't know what the young lovers thought or talked about in the hours leading up to their deaths. True victims and law enforcement names have been changed out of respect for the dead and the families of the victims.

As a teenager, I watched the partly true movie, *The Town that Dreaded Sundown*, and have always wondered whether The Phantom could have been a shell-shocked soldier returning from the war. That is the angle I've taken with this story and ask forgiveness for any fiction inserted into the reality of that horrible time.

I hope you enjoyed this first book in a series of unsolved crimes and urban legends set in Arkansas. If you did, please leave a review for *The Lovers' Lane Murders* and wait for the second book in *Secrets of the South*.

Thank you,

Cynthia Hickey

Don't miss the next story featuring Pressley and Jackson, coming soon, *The Prom Night Hitchhiker*, an urban legend about a dead girl who comes home once a year.

Arkansas Highway 365

Years ago, a young man was driving down Arkansas 365, south of Little Rock when he saw a young girl on the roadside. He offered to give her a lift and draped his coat over her shoulders because she was cold and soaked from the rain. She gave him directions to her house. When the young man got out and circled the car to the other side to help her out of her seat, no one was there. Confused, the man walked up to the house and knocked on the door. A woman answered, and he explained what had occurred. She said, "That young girl is my daughter, who was killed years ago. She hitchhikes back home once a year." The young man then drove to the cemetery to see the young girl's grave. There he found his coat draped over her tombstone.

THE
PROM NIGHT
HITCHHIKER
CYNTHIA
NEW YORK TIMES BEST-SELLING AUTHOR
HICKEY

Connect with me on FaceBook
Twitter
Sign up for my newsletter and receive a free short story

www.cynthiahickey.com

Follow me on Amazon
And Bookbub

Website at www.cynthiahickey.com

Multi-published and Amazon and ECPA Best-Selling author Cynthia Hickey has sold close to a million copies of her works since 2013. She has taught a Continuing Education class at the 2015 American Christian Fiction Writers conference, several small ACFW chapters and RWA chapters, and small writer retreats. She and her husband run the small press, Winged Publications, which includes some of the CBA's best well-known authors. She lives in Arizona and Arkansas, becoming a snowbird, with her husband and one dog. She has ten grandchildren who keep her busy and tell everyone they know that "Nana is a writer".

Enjoy other books by Cynthia Hickey

Secrets of Misty Hollow

CLEAN BUT GRITTY Romantic Suspense

Highland Springs

Murder Live
Say Bye to Mommy
To Breathe Again
Highland Springs Murders (all 3 in one)

Colors of Evil Series

Shades of Crimson
Coral Shadows

The Pretty Must Die Series

Ripped in Red, book 1
Pierced in Pink, book 2
Wounded in White, book 3
Worthy, The Complete Story

Lisa Paxton Mystery Series

Eenie Meenie Miny Mo
Jack Be Nimble

Hickory Dickory Dock

Brothers Steele
Sharp as Steele
Carved in Steele
Forged in Steele
Brothers Steele (All three in one)

The Brothers of Copper Pass
Wyatt's Warrant
Dirk's Defense
Stetson's Secret
Houston's Hope
Dallas's Dare
Seth's Sacrifice
Malcolm's Misunderstanding

Fantasy
Fate of the Faes
Shayna
Deema
Kasdeya

Time Travel
The Portal

Tiny House Mysteries

No Small Caper
Caper Goes Missing
Caper Finds a Clue
Caper's Dark Adventure
A Strange Game for Caper
Caper Steals Christmas
Caper Finds a Treasure

Wife for Hire – Private Investigators
Saving Sarah
Lesson for Lacey
Mission for Meghan
Long Way for Lainie
Aimed at Amy
Wife for Hire (all five in one)

A Hollywood Murder
Killer Pose, book 1
Killer Snapshot, book 2
Shoot to Kill, book 3
Kodak Kill Shot, book 4
To Snap a Killer
Hollywood Murder Mysteries

Shady Acres Mysteries
Beware the Orchids, book 1
Path to Nowhere
Poison Foliage
Poinsettia Madness
Deadly Greenhouse Gases

Vine Entrapment

Hearts of Courage
A Heart of Valor
The Game
Suspicious Minds
After the Storm
Local Betrayal

Overcoming Evil series
Mistaken Assassin
Captured Innocence
Mountain of Fear
Exposure at Sea
A Secret to Die for
Collision Course
Romantic Suspense of 5 books in 1

INSPIRATIONAL

Nosy Neighbor Series
Anything For A Mystery, Book 1
A Killer Plot, Book 2
Skin Care Can Be Murder, Book 3
Death By Baking, Book 4
Jogging Is Bad For Your Health, Book 5
Poison Bubbles, Book 6

CYNTHIA HICKEY

A Good Party Can Kill You, **Book 7 (Final)**
Nosy Neighbor collection

Christmas with Stormi Nelson

The Summer Meadows Series
Fudge-Laced Felonies, **Book 1**
Candy-Coated Secrets, **Book 2**
Chocolate-Covered Crime, **Book 3**
Maui Macadamia Madness, **Book 4**
All four novels in one collection

The River Valley Mystery Series
Deadly Neighbors, **Book 1**
Advance Notice, **Book 2**
The Librarian's Last Chapter, **Book 3**
All three novels in one collection

Historical cozy
Hazel's Quest

Historical Romances
Runaway Sue
Taming the Sheriff
Sweet Apple Blossom
A Doctor's Agreement
A Lady Maid's Honor
A Touch of Sugar

Love Over Par
Heart of the Emerald
A Sketch of Gold
Her Lonely Heart

Finding Love the Harvey Girl Way

Cooking With Love
Guiding With Love
Serving With Love
Warring With Love
All 4 in 1

A Wild Horse Pass Novel
They Call Her Mrs. Sheriff, book 1 (A Western Romance)

Finding Love in Disaster

The Rancher's Dilemma
The Teacher's Rescue
The Soldier's Redemption

Woman of courage Series

A Love For Delicious
Ruth's Redemption
Charity's Gold Rush
Mountain Redemption
Woman of Courage series (all four books)

Short Story Westerns

Desert Rose

<u>Desert Lilly</u>
<u>Desert Belle</u>
<u>Desert Daisy</u>
<u>Flowers of the Desert 4 in 1</u>

Contemporary

Romance in Paradise
<u>Maui Magic</u>
<u>Sunset Kisses</u>
<u>Deep Sea Love</u>
<u>3 in 1</u>

<u>Finding a Way Home</u>
<u>Service of Love</u>
<u>Hillbilly Cinderella</u>
<u>Unraveling Love</u>
<u>I'd Rather Kiss My Horse</u>

Christmas
<u>Dear Jillian</u>
<u>Romancing the Fabulous Cooper Brothers</u>
<u>Handcarved Christmas</u>
<u>The Payback Bride</u>
<u>Curtain Calls and Christmas Wishes</u>
<u>Christmas Gold</u>
<u>A Christmas Stamp</u>
<u>Snowflake Kisses</u>
<u>Merry's Secret Santa</u>
<u>A Christmas Deception</u>

The Red Hat's Club (Contemporary novellas)

Finally

Suddenly

Surprisingly

The Red Hat's Club 3 – in 1

Short Story

One Hour (A short story thriller)

Whisper Sweet Nothings (a Valentine short romance)